T0170671

Wonder World

WONDER WORLD

K.R. BYGGDIN

ENFIELD
&WIZENTY

Enfield & Wizenty
(an imprint of Great Plains Publications)
320 Rosedale Avenue
Winnipeg, MB R3L 1L8
www.greatplains.mb.ca

Great Plains Publications gratefully acknowledges the financial support provided for its publishing program by the Government of Canada through the Canada Book Fund; the Canada Council for the Arts; the Province of Manitoba through the Book Publishing Tax Credit and the Book Publisher Marketing Assistance Program; and the Manitoba Arts Council.

Design & Typography by Relish New Brand Experience
Printed in Canada by Friesens

Library and Archives Canada Cataloguing in Publication

Title: Wonder world / K.R. Byggdin.
Names: Byggdin, K. R., author.
Identifiers: Canadiana (print) 20220140332 | Canadiana (ebook) 20220140340 |
    ISBN 9781773370736 (softcover) | ISBN 9781773370743 (ebook)
Classification: LCC PS8603.Y49 W66 2022 | DDC C813/.6—dc23

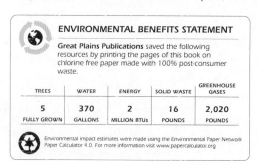

ENVIRONMENTAL BENEFITS STATEMENT

Great Plains Publications saved the following resources by printing the pages of this book on chlorine free paper made with 100% post-consumer waste.

TREES	WATER	ENERGY	SOLID WASTE	GREENHOUSE GASES
5	370	2	16	2,020
FULLY GROWN	GALLONS	MILLION BTUs	POUNDS	POUNDS

Environmental impact estimates were made using the Environmental Paper Network Paper Calculator 4.0. For more information visit www.papercalculator.org

Canadä

FSC
www.fsc.org
MIX
Paper from responsible sources
FSC® C016245

for Raynard, for everything

 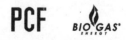

You don't talk to me
Not the way that you used to
Maybe I don't listen
In a way that makes you think I do
I've been wondering
About what we're gonna do
A house full of empty rooms
—*Kathleen Edwards*

1

The phone call from a man I never expected to hear from again comes on a cool Friday night in early July while I'm at Sobeys. A persistent dripping fog saturates Halifax, painting the city with a gloomy brush.

"Isaac? This is your …" A calculating inhalation of air. "This is Abraham. I have some news. Your grandfather has gone to be with the Lord."

I freeze. It feels like someone's taken an eggbeater to my intestines. By the time I find my voice again, he's already moved on.

"How did he—"

"There'll be—Sorry?"

"Nothing." I hold my breath, count to five in my head. "Go ahead."

"A service at the church. On Monday. If you wish to attend."

"Okay."

If I *wish?* That church is thirty-five hundred kilometres away and the last time we spoke, he told me I was banned from there for life.

I can't scan my groceries and catastrophize at the same time, so I abandon my place in line. Shrink back against the wall, clutching my shopping basket in front of me like a shield.

We're both quiet, absorbed in the strangeness of the moment. He breaks first.

"Well."

"Is that it then?" I ask.

My hand is cramping from the weight of the basket. It's exhausting to keep my defences up for this long.

"You're also to receive an inheritance."

I picture Opa Willie's well-used set of tools. The dogeared copy of *Martyrs Mirror* he kept above the toilet. His homemade knipsbrat board with the accompanying margarine container full of pieces.

"Oh? What is it?"

He clears his throat. "Wonder World."

All the images floating around my head burst, leaving only a howling void. Sweet Menno Simons on a bed of spätzle! Did I hear that right?

"Is that a joke?"

He makes one of those specific kinds of disapproving noises only Mennonites with wearisome children can produce from the back of their throats.

"No. The farm is yours, so long as you accept your grandfather's condition. Your aunt Deb can explain everything. She's the executor."

Neither of us knows how to end this somewhat surreal conversation, so we make awkward small talk about the weather and the price of gas for a couple of minutes before Abe says "Najo" and the call peters out. He doesn't offer to pay my way out to Manitoba, and I can't bring myself to ask.

The old man's words rattle around the inside of my head like change in the dryer as I step back into the self-checkout line to pay for my groceries. I don't go to the cashiers anymore. They all give me Pity-Eyes since I got caught trying to steal some beans and rice last month. The manager was real nice about it. She didn't call the cops or ban me from the store, just told me that her church had a food pantry open to anyone in need. I switched to self-checkout after that.

I key in the code for the cabbage I'll stir fry tonight with some of the soy sauce packets stuck to the back of the shared fridge in my apartment. Not a fancy supper, but at least it'll be good for me. Ever since one of my former roommates was diagnosed with scurvy after a year-long diet of instant ramen and store-brand cola, I've tried to eat as healthy as I can.

I should've checked the number before I picked up, but I was hoping my latest hookup-turned-hangout might be calling to make weekend plans. I didn't see the 204 area code flashing across the screen, and by the time I realized it was Abe, it seemed too late to back out. I've never been great with direct confrontation. I prefer to treasure up all my little grudges and ponder them in my heart for the rest of my life.

In a weird way, this out-of-the-blue glimpse into the life I left behind in Manitoba is kind of comforting. Like wading into a kiddie pool as an adult and realizing the water you once worried about drowning in only comes to your ankles.

I actually liked listening to the old man talk. Not what he was saying, but how he said it. The way he elongates every vowel and rolls each word around in his mouth like hard candy. Our conversation reminded me of what I've been missing these last ten years. Why Halifax has never quite felt like home. It's a transient city, a place where outsiders are supposed to visit but never settle down. No one sticks around here long enough to become your friend. My phone is full of contacts I know just well enough to get invited to their parties, but not enough to sustain a conversation for longer than five minutes if I actually show.

Sooner or later, everyone leaves the East Coast for greener pastures. Fort Mac or Montreal or maybe London if their parents are rich. The good London I mean, across the pond. Not the one in Ontario that feels like Winnipeg only sadder, which any Manitoban can tell you is a pretty remarkable achievement.

There's too much turnover here for someone like me who grew up in a place of deep-rooted prejudice and tradition. Mennoland is nothing if not stagnant. My people have been farming their little corner of the Prairies for generations, and their lives are just as cyclical as the growing season. Birth, drudgery, self-denial, death, repeat. With the next generation that is. Mennos definitely don't believe in reincarnation. One go around our kind of life is already more than most of us can take.

The power lines buzz with nervous energy as I navigate the store's soggy parking lot. Feels like I've got the city to myself the whole way back to the mouldering North End apartment I share with two randos I've taken to calling Bud and Dude because I can't remember their actual names. I could check the lease I guess, but there's a good chance none of us are on it. My landlord's not a real stickler when it comes to stuff like paperwork or maintenance. All he cares about is collecting our rent each month.

Which reminds me. I really should order some more cheques. The kind that don't bounce.

There's a veritable smorgasbord of all-you-can-pray holy houses sandwiched between the Sobeys and my place. The Orthodox church with its shiny copper roof. The Buddhist temple painted construction vest orange and guarded by two stone lions. The tidy red brick mosque that hosts the polling station I've forgotten to vote at during the last couple of elections. Whatever the Jehovah's Witnesses call the place they gather on weekends before heading out in pairs and offering doorside salvation services to hungover Haligonians paying penance for last night's beer and donairs.

This neighbourhood couldn't be more different from the town I grew up in, which had only one place to worship. I suppose technically there was also the United Church, but ever since word got out that their minister leads her congregation in a version of the Lord's Prayer that begins "Our Father *and Mother* who art in heaven," the place has been considered ecclesia non grata by most locals. Celestial gender bending is most decidedly frowned upon by the all-male leadership team at NMC, the Mennonite Brethren church on Main Street where Abe pastors.

Friend and foe alike have piled into that sanctuary every Sunday for as long as our town has existed. Even if we'd been arguing on Saturday. Even if we'd be talking behind each other's backs on Monday. Because our Jesus didn't get involved with those petty spats. He was looking at the big picture. The point was to make an effort once a week. Put on a smile and some nice clothes and plunk yourself in a pew for all to see so you could be counted as one of the faithful.

The thought of joining all those Judgemental Janzens for Opa's memorial service churns my stomach. Surely I could find a way to honour his memory out here. Cook up a box of frozen perogies and smother them in some schmauntfat made with bacon grease, cause you can't get proper farmer sausage on the East Coast. Block out the homesickness with a bit of heartburn.

Or I could rent a car and drive up to the wildlife park in Shubenacadie. It's sort of similar to Wonder World, the business my grandfather owned and operated on the edge of my hometown for almost half a century. Eighty acres of corn maze, U-Pick, petting zoo, and game farm built on land that generations of our family had grown crops and raised livestock on. "We bring the wonders of the world to your doorstep, and a smile to every face," Opa used to say. He kept everything from miniature goats to a pair of tiger brothers on the property, and there always seemed to be something new to see. As a kid, it was also the one place I felt unquestionably safe and understood because of my grandfather's easygoing and encouraging nature.

The realization that Opa Willie has left me this indelible landscape crackles through my body like lightning. Why would he do that? And what the heck am I supposed to do with it now?

My phone rings again, but I let it go to voicemail when I see my landlord's number. He sends a text almost immediately.

isaac your cheque didn't clear again - we need to talk

Or not? Talking's not going to change anything. It certainly won't make the money magically appear so I can cover this month's rent. Or last month's.

What have I got to show after a decade in Halifax? I've burned through every dating app and queer clique in this city. Dalhousie won't release my transcript until I pay off my account, but what's the point? Even if I wanted to take another crack at university, you can't transfer F's. I spent six years slowly flunking out of Dal's music program, and another four getting fired from a series of dead-end jobs that barely covered the cost of my increasingly precarious housing. I thought this city could be my new start, but instead I just keep spinning my wheels.

The landlord sends another text.

isaac i know you got my message - CALL ME

Fucking read receipts.

The truth is, there's nothing and no one keeping me here. If I return to Mennoland, I can say goodbye to Opa and take advantage of some good old-fashioned Christian charity to get back on my feet. My people love to help someone they can judge at the same time.

At home, I pick the least dirty pan out of the sink and fill it with hunks of cabbage I shred with my hands because I can't find our one good knife. I take in the cracks in the walls. The saggy water stain in the centre of the ceiling. The black mould sulking at the edges of the tiny window above the sink. A series of cruciferous farts emanates from the sizzling pan. Suddenly I'm not so hungry.

"Fine. Fuck it. I'll go."

I abandon the kitchen to Bud and Dude. They've never passed up a free meal, even when a container is clearly labelled with my name and *DO NOT TOUCH* in angry Sharpie. Let them squabble about whose turn it is to not do the dishes. I'm out of here.

It doesn't take long to pack my worldly possessions into a fraying traveller's backpack. I make a few trips to the nearest charity donation bins, returning anything that won't fit in my bag back to the thrift store from whence it came.

I'm able to hold it together until I realize I don't own any photos of Opa and me. Then the damn waterworks just won't stop. I thought it'd be easy enough to find one on Facebook, but apparently I've never posted about him in my feed. I keep scrolling and scrolling, working myself into a frenzy, desperate to find an image I can use to memorialize him on my profile. Not that many of my current stranger-friends on social media would have a clue who he is. Was.

Shit.

I put the phone down and draw my legs up onto my stripped second-hand mattress. Close my eyes. Picture Opa as I remember him, standing in one of his fields with a huge grin on his face as he tells me to lock my elbows and lifts me up off the ground with cracked and calloused hands. He was so strong and yet so gentle at the same time.

Once when I was a kid, I got nervous riding one of his horses and fell off. We weren't going fast, and I didn't really hurt anything other than my pride, but even so my initial shock quickly turned into wails and tears. Opa dropped whatever he was doing and came running. I never knew someone as old as him could run that fast. He picked me up, brushed the dirt off my forehead and knees, and sang his favourite hymn, "Gott Ist Die Liebe," to help me calm down.

"Just breathe, kjint," he kept saying as he rocked me in his arms.

Not "Don't cry" or "Be a man."

Just breathe.

If I could, I'd crawl inside that moment and never leave.

Unfortunately, the sound of my roommates enthusiastically murdering each other on the Xbox in the living room drags me back into the present. What will they say when they figure out I've left for good? Probably nothing. After all, ours was a Kijiji-blood-pact kind of arrangement. Three strangers pooling their meagre resources, clinging to life on the peninsula where all the good shows and bars and jobs are. It'll be easy for Bud and Dude to find someone else to rent the room. Drifters like me are a dime a dozen around here.

The landlord will likely call again because I didn't give three months' notice but I'm not asking for the damage deposit back so he's just going to have to deal. If there's one thing growing up in Mennoland taught me, it's that life's not fair.

2

Although I book the earliest flight I can find out of Canada's Ocean Playground, it takes nearly a day and a half before my sorry, jetlagged ass is finally deposited in Friendly Manitoba. I could have made the trip in a fraction of the time if I had the money to book with one of the big guys. Unfortunately, I was forced to travel with our nation's latest too-good-to-be-true low-cost carrier, Breezy Jet, purveyors of an ancient art known as Death by a Thousand Connecting Flights.

All these changing time zones and airport codes quickly turn my brain to mush. YHZ to YHM, YHM to YUL, YUL to YYC, YYC to YWG, WTF, SOS. I don't know how Breezy Jet is supposed to turn a profit by ping-ponging their hapless customers around the country like this. The fuel bill alone would be astronomical.

They must make all their money on the small stuff. We never seem to stop anywhere long enough for the passengers to disembark and grab some food, so we're forced to rely on the airline's expensive snacks for sustenance. I try to stay strong but end up caving on the third leg of the journey. Buy a three-dollar bag of peanuts from the flight attendant, then a five-dollar bottle of water to wash down the salt. Bastards.

When I finally stumble into the bathroom of the James Armstrong Richardson International Airport thirty-one hours later, the reflection in the mirror makes me wince. My wiry brown hair is plastered to my sweaty forehead, hiding how much it's receded over the previous decade. Yesterday's five o'clock shadow and the dark, sunken circles under my eyes give a harrowed edge to my round face. In short, I look like death warmed over. Maybe people will mistake me for the corpse at Opa Willie's funeral tomorrow.

A bible verse comes to mind. Something from Matthew. *When the disciples saw him walking on the lake, they were terrified. "It's a ghost," they said, and cried out in fear.* The thought of this makes me laugh and then swallow hard, because, you know, dead grandfather. Now is not the time to be making jokes.

I splash some water on my bloodshot eyes and descend the escalator to the futuristic arrivals area. The last time I flew out of Winnipeg it was through the old terminal building. It's amazing how discombobulating this cavernous new space is, especially the giant blue skylights hovering like UFOs high above me. I can't help but flinch when passing under the first one, expecting a beam to descend and suck me up into the sky. I miss the urine-like glow of the old airport's florescent lighting grid. That terminal somehow managed to feel both massive and claustrophobic at the same time. It was grungy and utilitarian, the perfect architectural metaphor for this hardscrabble Prairie city that sprawls out around the airport to the north, east, and south. When you stepped off the plane then, you knew what you were in for.

This new building presents a shiny, whitewashed Winnipeg that feels dishonest somehow. Like the city's ashamed of the past and wants the world to mistake it for something it's not. I get that, tried the same thing when I moved to Halifax. But it never works. Eventually, people always see through the polish to the pain you're hiding.

When I reach the bottom of the escalator, I bypass the hug rug full of jubilantly reuniting loved ones and head straight for the exit. My ride isn't waiting for me with balloons and a handmade *Welcome Home!* sign. No, Abe has informed me he'll be idling at the door so he doesn't have to pay for parking. Also, as a general rule, the Funk family aren't really huggers.

Beyond the revolving doors, the sweltering afternoon heat immediately engulfs me. Gone is the briny fishy air of the Maritimes, replaced by the scent of dirt clods and manure. Clouds squat over the city close and breathless, pressing me into the humid earth. I am a human hotdog, boiled with the plastic wrap still on. Bienvenue à Winnipeg, bitches.

Luckily, the old man's car is just a few steps away. He's still driving the same one all these years later: a bulbous, swampy-coloured Ford Taurus with a crooked bumper. It was me who dented it. Back in high school, while trying to figure out how to parallel park, during the only driving lesson Abe ever gave me. I mixed up the gas and break pedals, hopped the curb, and hit a hydro pole. He took the keys out of the ignition and didn't hand them back to me for months.

I wish Opa Willie could've picked me up. His ancient half-tonne didn't have AC, but he'd be waiting for me with rolled down windows and a huge grin. We'd spend the drive back to town catching up on my time away, our voices growing hoarse from laughing and shouting over the noise of the engine and the wind.

Instead, I half walk, half dog-paddle through the soupy air to Abe's car, hesitating just a second before deciding to get in the back. It would be cooler up front, but I can't stand the thought of being close enough to him that our elbows might touch.

Mercifully, he doesn't say anything as I manhandle my pack in behind the driver's seat and slide in next to it. Just cocks his head to one side. Maybe it was more of a twitch. A grimace? Jeez, I've forgotten how much I overanalyze things when I'm with this guy.

The old man shifts slightly in his seat. Not enough to turn around but enough for me to catch a flash of his frosty blue eyes in the rear-view. I look away, embarrassed by the intimacy of this momentary connection.

"Hello Abe."

His large pink hands squeeze the steering wheel for a moment. Then he nods.

"Buckle up," he replies before his eyes slip away from the mirror and back towards the road.

He pulls out onto the concrete jigsaw of Wellington Avenue. The tires make a familiar clunking sound over the cracks in the pavement, setting my teeth on edge. Abe cranks up the radio and AM 670, The Sound of the Southeast, fills the awkward hush seeping in between us. I recognize the program, *Heavenly Hymn Sing*. My aunt Gina would often tune in while she washed up our post-church-pot-roast dishes. The whole family used to gather for dinner every Sunday at her and Uncle Jake's place. Well, almost the whole family. My aunt Deb always claimed there was too much work to be done out at the farm, even though Opa Willie found the time to put in an appearance.

Shit. How is it Sunday already? If Abe had to book a back-up preacher to pick me up, he'll be annoyed. He's wearing his church suit, so maybe he just cut the sermon a little short and skipped after-service fellowship in the foyer. I can taste that scalding caffeinated sludge at the back of my throat.

Thankfully, there's an extra-large coffee from Timmy's and a crumpled paper donut bag wedged into Abe's cup holder, so that's one less reason for him to resent me. I'm jealous of the old man. He got to pregame this encounter with his beverage of choice and I didn't. I couldn't afford any of those tiny bottles of booze on the flights over here, so I'll need to conserve my energy until I can get to a liquor store. I want to ask him to stop somewhere in the city so I can stock up but don't because I can't stand the thought of the quiet judgement that would follow.

I close my eyes. Pretend to rest while I count the turns from the airport to Newfield, my hometown south of the city. It's not hard to do. There are only five. In Mennoland, even the roads are made to be straight.

One.

Two.

Something doesn't feel right. That was too early, wasn't it? I look up, frowning. Abe catches my face in the rear-view.

"Oh, that's right. You haven't been back in a little while. There's a new subdivision going up out past Linden Woods now. Had to rip up a bit of Waverley there. Extended Kenaston down to the Perimeter."

The old man certainly has the gift of understatement. I don't know anyone else who would call a whole decade of disconnect between parent and child "a little while." I blow a stream of exasperated air out through my cheeks, trying to be subtle about it, then close my eyes again. The long stretches of linearity continue, punctuated by the occasional turn.

Three.

Four.

The car starts to wind around a series of gentle curves. So, Abe's opted for St. Mary's Road over Highway 75. Guess he's not in much of a hurry to get back to town. That's fine. Neither am I.

The car slows down for a few minutes as we drive through Saint-Eustache-sur-la-Rivière, the French town halfway between Winnipeg and Newfield. A name too fancy for its own good. Everyone around here just calls it St. Stache.

Five.

The last turn before town. My hands are folded in my lap, fingernails digging deeper and deeper into skin. I try to focus on the pain instead of my thundering heart, but stop when I realize it might look like I'm praying.

Surveying Abe from behind, it's disturbing to realize just how much we're starting to look alike. Matching guts sag out in front of us. Our shoulders roll inwards in the same sort of self-protective slump. The only noticeable difference is our hair. His looks the same as always, like someone's driven a lawnmower through a straw field. Mine is more of a thick, unruly briar patch. Just like my mother's used to be, according to the few pictures I've seen of her. Loreena walked out on us a week after my second birthday, so I have no idea what she looks like these days.

From the tightening of his jaw and his clipped inhale of breath, I can tell without asking that he'd like me to shave off my stubble and get a haircut before the funeral. This is how we've learned to communicate with one another over the years, through mental osmosis. Listening to the space between words.

The old man snaps on the turn signal one last time. There's a familiar bump as we roll onto the driveway's chipped pavement. The house is painted the same sad shade of grey I recall from childhood. Abe presses the garage opener, and one of the doors creaks upwards to let us in. He exits the car with a grunt, and I follow him into the dated bungalow, both of us keeping our heads down out of habit to avoid looking at the other half of the garage. The side that's been empty since Loreena drove out of our lives for good.

"The bed's made up downstairs if you want a meddachschlop," Abe says over his shoulder as he heads towards the living room.

The sound of the television starts up almost immediately. Someone is singing about the sweet, satisfying love of Jesus. I resist the urge to make a comment about the lyrics' erotic undertones. Best to just disengage at this point.

Something painful pings in my chest as I take in my surroundings. These old wood-panelled walls. The overstuffed bookshelves full of bible commentaries and biographies of dead theologians. Abe's recliner with the faded corduroy fabric rubbed smooth under his feet. Everything looks exactly the same as it did on the day I left. This place is a sad museum, commemorating a part of my life I don't want to remember.

Slipping off my shoes, I place them next to the old man's in the mudroom, then move them again so there's a little gap between us. I make my way down the thinly carpeted stairs to the basement and find my old bedroom has been scrubbed of my existence. The walls have been repainted and most of the furniture is gone. All that's left is a twin bed, a small desk, and a folding chair. A single bare bulb sticks out of the ceiling, casting an interrogative glow over my spartan surroundings. Very prison cell couture.

Gone are all my movie posters and the stereo I used to blast after some teenaged argument with Abe. No, that's not quite right. Argument implies dialogue. While I might rage or plead with the old man about some injustice until my voice and tears were spent, he always sat there, quiet yet firm. Bricking himself off from my onslaughts with a wall of silence.

My bag is full of dirty clothes, so I dump whatever will fit into the basement washer before stepping into the downstairs bathroom. It'll be nice not to have a water bill for a while. I know the tiny hot water tank will struggle to cope with this double duty, but I don't mind a cold shower on a muggy day like this. Abe's got AC, but he prefers not to use it. Gives him an excuse to shut his curtains tight against the outside world.

When I turn on the taps in the shower, oily, overly softened well water spills over my head into my eyes and shoulders, making it hard to tell whether I have rinsed the shampoo out of my hair or not. The scent of old pennies and boiled eggs wafts out of the pipes and imprints itself on my skin. A Mennoland baptism.

Too late, I realize that all my whites will be stained orange with rust when I empty the machine, but I don't care. I am beyond caring.

Abe's show is still blaring down through the vents when I towel off in the bedroom. My arms feel like lead weights as I dry myself. I can't stop yawning. Have I ever been this tired before? Has anyone?

3

A pumpkin sky *hangs over the streets of Newfield, casting jack-o'-lantern shadows in the toothy gaps between houses. The entire town gathers on Main Street to trick-or-treat. Children and adults alike are dressed up in all kinds of terrifying costumes, from brain sucking zombies to alt-right trolls. We're marching through town together in a long, straight line, holding grocery bags out for candy, but without stopping at any of the homes we pass by. At some point I try to leave, but there are too many people jostling about and I'm swept along with the crowd.*

We end up at the church, men and boys on one side, women and girls on the other. I remain standing at the back of the room, unsure whether to stay or go. A side door at the front of the sanctuary opens and Opa Willie comes bounding out on stage. He's wearing a skeleton onesie and carrying an overflowing sack of candy. People cheer as my grandfather tosses them the brightly coloured treats. I call out to him in anticipation, eager to get my hands on some. Then someone brushes past me and rushes to the front of the room. It's Abe. He's the only one who hasn't dressed up. At least, I don't think his church suit counts as a costume. This makes sense, as he's always discouraged the celebration of Halloween. He's carrying a massive stack of bible tracts between his arms with tender reverence, as if cradling a sleeping baby. He moves among his congregation to confront them, knocking candy out of hands and stuffing tracts into the mouths of those who are already chewing. Gradually, the room grows still as Abe catches up to Opa and silences the crowd with his little booklets.

Soon I'm the only person left who hasn't received either candy or a tract. Opa and Abe seem to realize this at the same time. They converge on my location at the back of the room, each one thrusting their offering in my face. I want to reach out and take the candy from my grandfather more than anything else in the world, but I can't. Looking up, I find my hands stretched out and stuck high above me, each wrist affixed to a rough wooden plank with large metal spikes. It dawns on me I've been dressed as Jesus this whole time. My body is bloodied and bruised and I'm stark naked aside from a crown of thorns on my head. How did I not realize I was nailed to a fucking cross until now?

The wood is suddenly very heavy, and I buckle under its weight. Pain blooms up from every part of me. I scream at Abe, begging for his help to take away my cross, but the old man ignores me. He turns instead to Opa Willie, folding one of his papers into a tiny cube like communion bread and feeding it to his father. Abe turns Opa away from my suffering, offering him a seat among the congregation. My grandfather stops smiling and takes his place. Everyone stares straight ahead, unblinking.

I follow the crowd's gaze to the front of the room and that's when I see it. A glass box affixed to the pulpit with a large hammer inside. A hammer I could use to get these nails out of my hands. It's my only hope, but God this is going to hurt.

It takes an eternity to drag myself to the stage. The cross keeps getting snagged on the sanctuary's thick carpet, nails ripping deeper into my oozing, screaming flesh with each tug and jolt. All around me, heads begin to bow and hands are planted firmly on knees. No one gets up to assist me. The sound of many mouths opening and closing with the same steady rhythm reverberates through the sanctuary as the town chews on Abe's tracts.

When I reach the box, I try to smash it with the cross, but the glass is thick and unyielding. A note flutters down from the ceiling, landing face up on the floor in front of me.

FAITH THE SIZE OF A MUSTARD SEED REQUIRED TO BREAK GLASS.

"But I don't have that!" I say, panicking.

Someone joins me on stage. There's blood in my eyes, but I know it's Abe. I move towards him, a pleading look on my face. He smiles and reaches out a helping hand.

I open my mouth to thank him and something snaps towards me. It's a tract. Abe's stuffing it down my throat. The paper rapidly expands inside me, choking all the air out of my lungs.

"Why?" I want to ask him. "Why would you do this to me? Why won't you help?"

But the words won't come out. All I can do is scream inside my skull as the old man lifts me up to the wall, tenderly adjusting the cross until I hang perfectly straight. He turns away from me and walks down the aisle. The lights in the sanctuary blink out row by row behind him. In the darkness, a thousand glowing pairs of eyes stare up at me, unblinking and unmoved by my frozen, public agony.

I wake in a cold sweat to find a basket of folded laundry outside my bedroom door. Abe must have put my clothes in the dryer. Another one of his little intrusions.

It feels unbelievably good to put on a clean shirt before heading up the stairs to the kitchen. The television has finally been silenced and the old man's door is closed, so I guess it's his turn to rest.

My stomach asserts itself with a growl, reminding me that I've yet to eat today. I reach for a cupboard door. It opens with a loud creak, and my hand recoils before I can see what's inside. Would Abe be okay with me eating his food? We never really worked out the details of my stay here. Maybe it's best for me to fend for myself until he says otherwise.

The clock on the kitchen stove reads 4:15. Good. I still have forty-five minutes before the only grocery store in town closes. I slip on my shoes and head outside, making sure to swipe a spare house key. I wouldn't put it past Abe to forget I'm here and lock me out.

4

Walking to the store, I'm reminded how much Mennoland values simplicity. All along Main Street our businesses are branded with straightforward signs: Flatlander Feeds, Southeast Credit Union, Countryside Co-op Gas Bar. Then there's the name of the town itself. We used to have a Plautdietsch one, something about a meadow full of flowers, but then the First World War happened and people started to worry that it sounded "too German." Our farmers didn't want any of their buyers to mistake us for friends of the Kaiser, so a group of local men was tasked with picking a new name, something English. After much prayer and discernment, the committee sent a letter off to the Manitoba government and erected a new welcome sign. We've been saddled with Newfield ever since.

I was so pissed when I first heard that story at school. I mean, how many towns get a do-over on their name? We could have called ourselves absolutely anything and the brightest minds we had picked Newfield. Newfield! My people have absolutely no sense of imagination.

Still, even I have to admit it's kind of apropos. The world around this town does unfold like a patchwork quilt smoothed over the endless mattress of the earth. We are just one new field planted alongside hundreds more. Blue flax. Yellow canola. Green cornstalks. Black asphalt and roof shingles.

When I reach the grocery store, I grab a metal shopping cart just to have something cold to rest my elbows against after the sweltering walk and head straight for the meagre liquor section. Newfield made national news when they finally voted to go wet five years ago, one of the last towns in the province to do so. Even I heard about it all the way out on the East Coast. Even so, I notice the middle-aged guy pacing anxiously up and down the booze aisle won't make eye contact with me as I roll up to the boxed wines. Old sins die hard, I guess.

Like Abe's place, the store looks exactly how I remember it. Same dusty flickering fluorescents overhead. Same polished puke-green tiles underfoot. Does nothing ever change around here?

After picking up the cheapest box of red I can find, I saunter to the back of the store to grab tortilla chips, store-brand alfredo sauce, a jar of dill pickles, and some cheese slices. Tonight's supper is going to be a Newfield classic: nasty nachos. It may sound disgusting, but ever since Neth and I invented this conglomeration of processed perfection during a late-night raid of her parents' kitchen back in grade seven, I've been hooked. The stuff is tasty and cheap as borscht. The perfect comfort food.

Thinking about my childhood bestie and our rebellious antics, I'm seized by a sudden urge to ride my cart down the aisle. Unfortunately, a little old lady appears out of nowhere just as I hit peak speed. The woman's shopping basket is filled to the brim with severely dented soup cans, each of them bearing a large, red *DISCOUNTED* sticker. I swerve to avoid her and the cart nearly tips.

"Sorry about that!" I say, flashing an apologetic grin. "Caught up in the spirit, I guess."

"Du schludonnst," she mutters, shaking her head.

I don't know much Plautdietsch, just a handful of phrases I gleaned from Opa over the years, but it's clear from her tone that she's not impressed.

To make up for my little disturbance, I let her go in front of me when we round the corner to the cash register. She smiles at this, then spots the box of wine I've plunked down behind her and sucks her teeth in reproach. I keep my eyes glued to the floor as I scoop up the cart's other contents and dump them behind the booze, feigning interest in some discounted paraphernalia left over from Canada Day while I wait for the cashier to ring me through.

The woman hands over a crumpled five for all the dented cans and shuffles off towards the parking lot, her bags bulging with half-priced booty. When it's my turn to pay, the cashier asks for my ID in a rehearsed, monotone way and I rummage in my wallet for my Nova Scotia driver's licence. When I hand it to her, our eyes connect and there's a flash of recognition. We both say "It's you!" at the same time.

She eyes my nasty nacho supplies and gives a knowing smirk. "So, Funk. Still a man of questionable tastes I see."

"Hey, Chicky, good to see you!"

She scans the box of wine and double bags it. "I didn't know you were back in town."

"Yeah, guess we've got some catching up to do!" I say, catching sight of the obvious baby bump under her red store apron.

"For sure."

She grins, and just like that we're back in high school again. It's Neth. Aganetha Kehler. My Paraguayan partner-in-crime since kindergarten, when her family moved in across the street. My stargazing, beer-chugging, menthol-smoking, hell-raising former best friend is standing in front of me and it's like I was never gone.

Except I was, for a really long time, and now she's Aganetha Giesbrecht, with two kids and apparently a third on the way. Wait. Does that mean we're supposed to be the responsible adults in the room now? Jesus. Must have missed that memo.

Neth's mousy hair is pulled up into a tight bun that stretches her features in an unpleasant way. Every so often she winces and shifts her weight onto the other foot. She looks exhausted. If I'd seen her on the street, I might have mistaken her for her mother.

When we were teenagers, Neth would often show up for school a couple of minutes after "O Canada" with that Just Rolled Out of Bed look: Tweety Bird pajama pants, a pair of Vans skater shoes she wore like slippers with the heels squashed down, and a hoodie that was two sizes too big for her. She never bothered with makeup or her hair, which was usually matted from her pillow and streaked with green or purple highlights she achieved with a shaken up can of silly string. Still, she'd greet me with a mischievous grin before knocking back a few grape or watermelon Nerds, her breakfast of choice. If a teacher ever called her out on her tardiness, she was always ready with a quick retort that made the whole class laugh.

It's hard to tell if that carefree kid exists inside this weary adult. For a second, I study her face, expecting her to toss her apron and run off with me somewhere to get shit-faced and catch up. But of course that's not an option. Neth's a working mom now. Her time is spoken for. So instead my hands fall limply at my sides and she has to tell me three times that I can have my ID back before I take it from her and pay using a credit card I should have cut up months ago.

I grab my bags and do my best to sound casual. "So hey, I'm actually going to be in town for a while."

"Really?" She pauses in the middle of handing over my groceries, eyebrows raised in surprise. "I figured you'd be out of here as soon as the funeral was over."

"You heard about Opa?"

She shrugs. "It's Newfield."

Ah, small towns. I'd forgotten what it's like to live in a place where everyone knows your business. I used to hate that in high school, but right now? It's kind of nice. It's been a while since anyone cared enough to keep tabs on me. I had to take the express bus to the airport. There was no one in Halifax I could think of to ask for a ride.

"Maybe we could hang out sometime?" I ask. "If you're not too busy. Well, I know you probably are. I just mean, like, no pressure or anything."

"I'd love that," she says, ignoring my awkward rambling.

Something flickers inside me. A hopeful something. I nod like a bobblehead. "Me too."

"Hey, I'm sorry about your opa," Neth says. "He was a cool guy. I actually took my kids to Wonder World a bunch before it closed down. They loved it there. Willie always gave them free pellets to feed the ducks."

"I didn't realize it closed."

"Yeah, five years ago. When Willie moved into Sunset Villa. You're sure out of the loop, aren't you Funk?" she adds, seeing the astonishment on my face.

"I guess. That's nice your kids liked going though," I say, trying to sound breezy. "How old are they now?"

"Nine and six."

Holy shit! "Wow."

"Yep. And about three months until we meet the newest member of the family," she says, giving her belly a pat.

"That's so crazy. I never pictured you as a mom."

God. If I had a free hand, I'd be cramming it in my mouth.

"Sorry," I say. "That came out wrong. What I meant was—"

I'm interrupted by a pointed cough from behind. The store seems to have filled up in the last couple of minutes. Half a dozen people are in line now, each of them shifting heavy shopping baskets full of dented cans from hand to hand. Word must have spread about the soup sale. If I had any friends left in Halifax, I'd take a picture and send it to them. I don't know how to explain it exactly, but this tableau really sums up Mennoland.

"Better let you go, Chicky. Don't want to hold up the soup brigade."

"I fucking hate discount days," she mutters.

There she is! The Neth I used to know. I move out of the way and smile goodbye, but her eyes have already glazed over as she turns to the next customer in line.

There are no traffic lights in Newfield, so I have to wait for a gap in the cars before I can cross Main Street. Standing on the curb, I notice a nearby stop sign has been altered with some spray paint to read *STOP DRINKING*. A fellow artist, or perhaps the same one, has labelled an abandoned milk tanker rusting out in the empty lot across the street as *SOUR CREAM*. I guess this is what passes for graffiti in Mennoland. We've never been very good at thinking outside the box around here.

Walking back to Abe's place, weighed down by the double-bagged wine and food in my hands, I can't stop thinking about something stupid. The time Neth and I kissed.

It only happened once, on a warm June night two weeks before our high school graduation. We were lying in a field somewhere on the edge of town. Waiting for a meteor shower or a lunar eclipse or something. It was after midnight, and we were piss-drunk off a case of cheap beer Neth got her cousin to pick up from St. Stache.

We'd been talking shit for hours, like we always did back then. Eventually, the conversation circled around to our post-high school plans.

"Will you still remember your best friend when you're a big famous penis performing for the rich and famous?" Neth asked, tracing imaginary constellations across the sky with a sloppy finger.

I was mid-swig and almost sprayed a mouthful of beer in her face. "I think you mean *pianist*, Neth. I'm going into music, not porn."

"Oh, right." She giggled. "My bad."

"I'll fly home at Christmas. Maybe Thanksgiving too. You won't even notice I'm gone. Trust me."

Neth lets her arm drop down to her stomach. "This town is going to fucking suck without you, Funk."

Her response was whispered, so I wasn't sure if she'd meant for me to hear it. I tossed my empty into the grass. Tracked the blinking light of a satellite orbiting overhead.

It was hard to know how to respond. The truth was our friendship was rapidly approaching its first big fork in the road, and neither one of us could say for sure how often our paths would link up from here on out. The future had been a touchy subject for us ever since I'd been accepted to Dalhousie on a full scholarship. Unfortunately, none of the schools Neth applied to had offered her any cash. Her parents didn't have a college fund she could tap into; they had their hands full just keeping food on the table for six kids. She had her part-time job at the grocery store, but that was only minimum wage. So while I'd be jetting off to Halifax on someone else's dime, she'd be stuck in Newfield picking up shifts and dreaming of her own way out for at least another year or two.

I felt the tip of Neth's pinky touch mine and looked over to find her staring at me. There was something swirling just out of reach behind her eyes. Something important. I opened my mouth, but she cut me off before I could pose my question.

"Did you hear Sara Dirks and Tommy Harms got engaged last night?"

"Oh my God!" I shouted, reeling away from her in mock horror. "No way."

"Yes way! My cousin saw them at the Sals on Pembina. Him and Tommy's brother are friends, so he recognized him straight away." She fumbled around for a new beer and cracked it open, downing a good third of the can before going on. "Apparently Tommy got the waitress to spray some whipped cream over the ring before she brought out dessert. Like, how fucking tacky can you get? And they're both still living at home yet! Probably had to borrow his dad's credit card to pay the jeweller."

"No way," I scoffed. "Do you think Sara will be wearing the ring at grad?"

"Oh, one hundred percent! It's all she'll want to talk about from now on. How *romantic* her *fiancé* is. How *perfect* the *big day* is going to be. Makes me want to barf."

I thought about all the people in town I knew who had gotten hitched at eighteen. How many sixtieth and even seventieth wedding anniversaries our church had hosted over the years.

Mennoland had long been the undisputed marriage capital of Canada. What else could you expect from horny teenagers whose parents kept telling them the altar was the only way to access the garden of earthly delights?

I propped myself up on one elbow and grabbed another beer. "Ten bucks says Tommy books them a honeymoon suite in Fargo, and the hotel has to offer them sparkling cider instead of free champagne cause they're underage."

Neth snickered and joined in. "Twenty bucks says Sara buys a white grad dress to cut down on costs."

"Fifty bucks says she'll have a ten-pound 'preemie' six months later!" I said, using air quotes and breathing through the laughter that burst out of my gut. "It's gotta be a shotgun wedding for sure, hey?"

I waited for a response, but Neth had gone quiet. I sat up again and put a hand on her shoulder, but she wouldn't look at me.

"Hey, what's up?"

For a second it seemed like she might cry. I started to apologize, though I didn't know what for. Neth stopped me. Reached up with both her hands, pulled my head down to hers. Kissed me. Hard. Not with her tongue or anything, but like, our teeth connected. It lasted about a minute. Then she got up and stumbled off in the direction of her house.

That moment between us, it wasn't sexual or anything. We loved each other a lot back then, but not in that way. I guess Neth just realized before I did that our time was up and decided to kiss our childhood goodbye.

As kids, we always told each other everything. There was no problem we couldn't fix with a bike ride around town and a swamp slushie from the Co-op: frozen layers of 7-Up, Pepsi, Orange Crush, and Dr. Pepper we sucked back with matching neon straws. Neth was the first person I came out to, and when her DIY belly ring got infected in grade nine, I helped her care for it so she wouldn't have to fess up to her parents. That day in the field was the first time she didn't tell me what was wrong.

I found out about her marriage to Connor Giesbrecht while scrolling through Facebook in my Halifax dorm room that fall. The birth of their first kid followed a few months after that. I had no idea they'd been seeing each other, or at least fooling around. Maybe she thought I'd judge her for fucking a homophobic Neanderthal like Connor. I don't know, I probably would have. That guy was a huge asshole to me ever since our first day of school. She could've done so much better than him. Than anyone in Newfield. Still, I should've been there for her. I should've skipped school and flown back as soon as I heard the news. But I was too chickenshit. And then it was ten years later.

In my experience, there are only two ways to survive this town. You either get in or get gone. I don't blame Neth for the choice she made. I just wish she'd had another option.

It's not until five or six hours later, as I'm lying in bed regretting the baking pan of nasty nachos and the half box of wine I've inhaled, that the idea comes to me. Abe hasn't shown his face since getting back from the airport and I've been going stir-crazy in his basement.

I enter the ten digits into my phone by heart, smearing a bit of forgotten alfredo sauce from my thumb on the cracked screen. There aren't many phone numbers I still have memorized, but I was there at the MTS kiosk in the St. Vital mall when this one was handed out to a giddy teenager who'd just cashed her first paycheque. I know it's a long shot, but just this once, I'm hoping the static nature of this town will work in my favour and the number hasn't changed. I take a deep breath and type a message to my new contact.

hey this is fuck :)

Goddamn autocorrect! I mash at the keyboard again.

I mean fork

What the hell?

FUNK!!

There. But which Funk? Perhaps I should clarify.

I S A A C
Funk=Isaac
me
:/

Seriously, dude. How many Funks would Neth know with a 902 number? Okay, just chill. It's fine. Don't freak yourself out.

Too late. All my blood pools into my extremities as soon as I exhale. I pause for a moment as my pulse ripples through my ear lobes and toes. Try to think of something intelligent to say next.

wat does it feel like to give birth?? like REALLY

I want to delete these words as soon I've typed them, but I've already hit send.

Shit. My brain ratchets up into true panic mode. What if this isn't Neth's cell anymore? Or worse, what if it is?

I lurch out of bed and then immediately tumble back down again because the room is suddenly spinning. The congealed mass of wine-soaked nachos in my gut threatens to transform the wall beside me into a Jackson Pollock painting. I crumple to the floor and lie there for a few minutes, feeling angry and sorry for myself at the same time. Then my phone vibrates in my hand. I brace myself for Neth's inevitable Fuck Off message.

But lo! What's this? A string of jumbled letters and numbers. What does it mean? Oh. I see. A URL. I tap the link and it takes me to a clip of the chest-burster scene from *Alien*. I laugh so hard I get a stitch in my side. Another message pops up on my screen.

Actual footage of me in the St. Stache delivery
room last time around. No joke, hurts like a mother!

Pun intended, haha. but worth it! :) :) Now do
yourself a favour Funk...lay off the wine and get
some sleep! Big day tomorrow for u.

She knows me too well. Speaking of Opa's funeral, I should probably pick up a Gatorade at the Co-op on my way to church tomorrow. And some Gravol. Okay, and maybe a pair of sunglasses too. Look out Newfield, the prodigal son is back in town.

5

I wake to the late morning light streaming in through the bedroom's grimy window. My eyes refuse to open more than a sliver, so I'm reduced to feeling around my bag for something to throw on. It seems like every step up from the basement is a mini-Everest, but I manage to drag myself to the kitchen where Abe is bending over the table and writing a note. He's looking quite rumpled in his Sunday suit and very possibly the same shirt and tie as yesterday. Did he sleep in those clothes?

He straightens up quickly when he hears me on the stairs, wrinkling his nose in displeasure at the smog of booze, plastic cheese, and sweat that accompanies me. I wish I could bottle this look. It's one hell of a hangover cure.

Abe's eyes widen as he takes me in. It's only now that I realize I'm wearing my kimono. Well done, Funk. The robe is made of green silk with a series of chopsticks and sushi rolls printed all over it. I found it at this quirky little store on Gottingen Street in Halifax that specialized in second-hand clothes, old board games, and taxidermy. When I caught sight of one gaudy sleeve sticking out from the rack, I knew it was destiny.

Abe is not looking at my robe, however. No, he's zeroed in on the hairy nipple falling out of it. The one I had pierced sometime during the boozy haze of frosh week my first year at Dal.

I clutch at the slippery fabric and pull it closed before croaking out "Good morning."

"Wasn't sure whether to wake you," the old man says, abruptly looking away. "Thought I'd head over to the church a bit early. There's a viewing from noon until two and the family is gathering at one o'clock in one of the Sunday school rooms for a time of prayer and reflection. But perhaps you'd like to just come for the service?"

"Yeah, I'll be there at two."

Making small talk with my extensive network of right-wing relatives in a confined space is my personal definition of hell on earth. Abe looks visibly relieved by my decision.

"Shall I save you a seat with us?" he asks, casually scratching at some nonexistent speck of dirt on his lapel.

I picture the deluge of gossip that would surge around me on my way to the front row.

Is that the Funk boy?

Who?

You remember, the homosexual. Or half-homosexual? Anyway, the one our poor pastor was forced to disown a decade ago.

Oh, that one! Well. I'm surprised he'd show his face here after everything he's put his family through.

"Naw, I'll be fine on my own, thanks."

Abe gives a sharp nod, as if to say "that's what I was thinking too" and fiddles with his tie. "Well. Maybe we can. You know. After the service?"

Speak plainly Abraham. What do you want? To catch up? Say you're sorry? Double check that my sexuality still has me damned for all eternity? Spit it out.

I shrug and weakly echo his "maybe" in response. We both know I came back to Newfield for Opa, not him.

He heads for the door, eyes firmly fixed on the linoleum floor. I hear the Taurus start up, which is weird, because the house is less than two blocks from the church. Guess he wants to remove any temptation I might have to blow off the service and go for a joyride.

I walk over to the table and read Abe's note. His handwriting has gotten shakier in the last ten years, but it's still legible.

Gone to NMC (Newfield Mennonite Church). There's coffee in the pot but I had to unplug the machine (in case of fire). The mug on the counter is microwave safe (if it's gone cold). Out of cereal (sorry).

It's the brackets that really get me. Clearly my old man's leaving nothing to chance here. How brain-dead does he think I am? Like I would ever forget the name of the church he excommunicated me from.

That's when I spot the nacho pan soaking in the sink, bits of processed cheese hanging down from the sides like so many tiny stalactites. I might have left it on the stove last night, or maybe the carpet outside my room, but definitely not here. I let go of the robe with a sigh. Yet another mess Abe had to clean up for me.

There is a neatly folded square of newsprint beside his note. It's from last Thursday's copy of *The Weekly Word*, our local paper. Opa Willie is smiling up at me from the page. It's an older photo, but he's still very recognizable in his usual uniform of coveralls and large rubber boots. Two ducks are tucked under his arms. They almost look to be smiling as they gaze up at him. I wouldn't be surprised if they were. Opa always did have a special way with animals.

Unfortunately, a quick scan through the clipping shows that his obituary is a lot less interesting than the photo. It reads like someone printed off the first generic template they could find online and filled in the blanks.

William "Willie" Funk ... loving husband, father, and grandfather ... predeceased by his beloved wife Gertrude "Trudy" in 1968 ... remembered by his children Jacob (Regina), Abraham, Deborah, and their families.

I guess *and their families* is supposed to cover me, his only grandchild.

This must have been written by my aunt Gina. She always makes a big show of using peoples' full names, even though no one around here has ever called her "Regina." Newfielders don't generally take too kindly to "folks putting on airs" as Opa used to say.

The obit manages to take all the fun out of my grandfather's life, which is too bad because he had a lot of it. Even his career is described in a humdrum way.

> *Prior to his retirement, William was a skilled farmer and caretaker of a local game farm.*

There's no mention of the twin Siberian tiger cubs Opa bought from a bankrupt circus in the mid-seventies, or the elderly giraffe that turned heads as it grazed alongside a country highway in the middle of the Prairies. My grandfather put this town on the map when he opened Wonder World, attracting thousands of visitors to Newfield each year. Evidently, some of my family feel this is not worth remembering. Instead Opa's life has been boiled down to a couple of barebones paragraphs and two dates tied together on the page.

> *March 12, 1930–June 29, 2018.*

Wait a second. If Opa died June 29, that means Abe waited a whole week before tracking me down. If I hadn't been in the will, would he have even bothered to let me know at all? It feels like someone's inflating a beach ball in my chest that could burst at any moment. Where exactly did I fit in Abe's list of to-dos after Opa passed?

1. Call funeral home to collect body.
2. Set out underwear, socks, shirt, suit, and shoes for the mortician to dress your dad in. Change your mind several times about the tie, then finally place three options in a grocery bag and have someone else choose.

3. Select dignified but reasonably priced coffin with siblings.
4. Accept casseroles and condolences from congregation.
5. Pack grief up into several good-sized boxes and stack unlabelled in the back of the crawlspace above the garage.

.

.

.

492. Call estranged son at last possible second after first calculating how to tell him that his grandfather is dead using the fewest words possible. Hang up before discussing important details such as flights, funeral arrangements, reconciliation. Wait for him to text you about (some) of these things later. Avoid thinking about the last ten years as you loop around the airport arrivals area again and again and again, waiting for him to land, burning up fuel just to save a few bucks on parking.

I fume at the old man in my head while rummaging through my backpack for a suitable ensemble that won't raise too many eyebrows. Finally, I settle on a wrinkled blazer over a plain white button-up and some dark grey chinos that drown me. I'd rather wear something with a skinny leg, but that would probably give some of my fellow funeralgoers a heart attack. If I'm going to go to this thing I need to blend in, and that means looking respectfully shapeless. In Mennoland, men's fashion is generally limited to items that make you look like you've recently lost thirty pounds but haven't had time to shop for a new wardrobe yet.

Still, I can't help pulling out one small statement piece for my look: a pair of black oxfords with a white, chunky heel that someone's deliberately speckled all over with flecks of gold and silver paint. Another brilliant thrift store find in Halifax. University towns are so deliciously odd.

When everything is laid out, I return to the kitchen and run the tap until it's cold. I fill up the mug Abe's left for me and knock back a mouthful of water, trying to ignore the way its metallic tang makes me feel like I'm drinking blood, then sit down at the table and sip slowly until I come back to the world.

I'd prefer some tea, but there's only Abe's coffee on the counter. There used to be a whole bunch of mint growing in our backyard. Maybe it's still there, I don't know. My aunt Deb would get me to pick some with her every summer. Showed me how to dry it out and boil the leaves for tea. She said my mother planted it when she and Abe first moved here. That she always kept a pot of mint tea brewing for any guests that might pop by back in the day.

Deb and I stored our leaves in a decorative tin beside the stove. It was a winter scene à la Thomas Kinkade: three people building a snowman together. They were all smiling and rosy cheeked. Behind them was a cozy cottage, wisps of smoke curling up from its chimney to join the perfectly puffy clouds in the sky. I used to take it down from the cupboard and stare at it sometimes when I was little. Imagine me, Abe, and Loreena as one happy family, just like the one on the tin. Obviously, that was a stupid dream. These days, I buy my tea from a store.

I pass the time by watching hummingbirds flit around a feeder Abe has suction-cupped to the outside of the big kitchen window. It's a strangely cheery scene, at odds with the house's overall tomblike vibe. Occasionally, I glance at the clock on the stove to make sure I won't be late for Opa's funeral. Thirty minutes, an hour, two and a half hours pass. I delay my departure until I'm sure the service will start just as I slip into the back row. Churches are like nuclear meltdown zones for me these days. It doesn't take long to get beyond my safe exposure limit.

I avoid the disposable razor and comb the old man's set out for me in the downstairs bathroom and leave my hair a frizzled rat's nest. Call it a little pacifist-aggressive protest against Pastor Abe, a man who's always been more worried about appearances than feelings.

There's a part of me that wants to go into all the rooms in the house before I leave and turn on each light just to run up his hydro bill, but I don't. I do lock the front door, even though everybody in town's going to be at this funeral and Abe's got nothing worth stealing. It's just what he expects. The baking sheet remains in the sink, unwashed.

6

It's a minor miracle I don't burst into flames when I step over the threshold of Newfield Mennonite Church. The board of elders made it quite clear I was no longer welcome here after Abe caught me making out with Noah Enns on grad night.

I was riding pretty high that day. All my hard work had finally paid off, and I'd earned my golden ticket out of Mennoland. I had the highest average, the biggest scholarships, and the brightest future of anyone in my class.

In Newfield, every major event from weddings to funerals to high school graduations is held at NMC. When I took Abe's pulpit to deliver my valedictory address, it felt like the whole church, the whole town was applauding for me. Some of the church ladies serving refreshments had even clipped out my feature in *The Weekly Word* and asked for my autograph after the ceremony.

At eight o'clock that evening there was a dance at the school gym, a recent addition to graduation festivities Principal Nickel had reluctantly permitted after years of pleading and cajoling from his students. We were all ecstatic. They left the lights on, and a dozen sharp-eyed chaperones prowled the perimeter of the dance floor to make sure we all left room for Jesus during the slow songs, but still. We were in the school almost after dark, with an actual DJ playing actual secular music, except for the songs on Principal Nickel's banned list. It was the closest to a normal teenager experience any of us awkward Anabaptists ever got, and it was glorious.

I could feel freedom blowing through me like a cold wind. When Neth invited me to pregame the dance with her, I figured she must have shaken off that night in the field. We sat in the shadows on the far side of the schoolyard, giggling on the swing set as we downed our usual party pump-up drinks, which in those days was a bottle of Sour Puss Blue chased down with a six pack of Smirnoff Ice. Our world was already blurry by the time we entered the gym, and it grew blurrier as we passed a smuggled flask between ourselves at the back of the bleachers. It was risky to let my freak flag fly during such a large, official gathering, but I thought none of these people's opinions were going to matter once I was at college. My tightly wound public persona of the studious pastor's kid caught a snag, and I was quite happy to let the whole thing unravel.

Abe was there too. He'd volunteered to stand around looking mildly miserable, checking purses and jackets for contraband. This included, apparently, not only drugs and booze but also condoms and, according to a few of the girls, any "provocative" shades of lipstick he came across. I was mortified and did my best to ignore him the whole night.

At some point I left for a discreet smoke break and Noah Enns followed me out.

"Can I have one?" he asked, gesturing to my cherry-flavoured Captain Blacks.

"Sure," I said, grinning at this adorable act of late-stage rebellion.

I knew how to let loose when the adults weren't looking, but Noah was the most strait-laced kid in my grade. He never once badmouthed a teacher, skipped class, or cut in front of someone on pizza day, and he most definitely did not attend any of our weekend bush parties.

Noah was also totally gay, but so deeply closeted he was practically in Narnia. He probably thought no one noticed how the tips of his ears would turn bright red whenever another boy got too close in gym or when our band teacher, the one with the perpetually half-buttoned dress shirts, leaned over his music stand to answer a question and gave our class a glimpse of his sexy chest fur.

Except I noticed, because I was playing the same game he was. In fact, Noah was the only queer-curious classmate I hadn't managed to make out with by the end of grade twelve. It was kind of a disappointment, actually. So imagine my surprise and delight when the final holdout on my booty bingo card wanted to bum one of my smokes.

"Nice speech earlier," he offered, chewing on a chapped lip. "You must be pretty excited about Halifax, eh?"

"For sure," I said. "No looking back."

He nodded, eyes never quite meeting mine.

We lingered outside. The lighter kept going out in his shaking hands even though there was no wind. He'd obviously never done this before. Finally, I put him out of his misery. Took the cigarillo and lit it for him. When I tried to pass it back though, Noah didn't take it. I noticed he was kind of staring at me then. Trembling a little.

I asked him what was wrong. We were close. I could feel his breath on my cheek. And then he pulled me towards him. Everything was suddenly all fingers and tongues and flushed skin and it was amazing, it was the best, it was perfect. Until it wasn't.

Because he was there, somehow. Abe. Calling my name. Pulling us apart. Dragging me home.

It could just as easily have been a girl he caught me with. At worst, the night might have ended with a minor talking to about the importance of pre-marital purity. Or maybe not even that. The old man tended to ignore my private indiscretions for the most part. Except Noah wasn't a girl. And this time, Abe wasn't going to look the other way.

A special elders meeting was convened at NMC. The same people who had been celebrating my success a day earlier now stared at me with suspicion and contempt. My summer was supposed to be one slow, smug victory lap around this tired old town, but now I'd have to slink away in shame.

They interviewed me and Noah separately. I've had ten years to forgive him for what he did. Telling them it was all my fault. That it was me who kissed him. That I forced myself on him.

I know he was just trying to survive. We all were. But still. He hung me out to dry. So fuck him. Fuck him all the way back to Ecuador or Laos or wherever the fuck the Mennonite Disaster Service has him stationed these days. The important thing is he kissed me first. Whatever people say.

The whole town has turned out for Opa Willie's service. Hundreds of folks have packed into the church by the time I arrive and more are pouring in by the minute. Funeral-going has always been a spectator sport in Newfield. It's partially on account of the faspa meal everyone is served after the service, a cornucopia of all our favourite comfort foods like cold cuts, cubes of Bothwell cheese, and assorted dessert squares. Lamentation and a free lunch are essential ingredients for a good social gathering in Mennoland.

Extra seating has been set up in the foyer. I squeeze past a long row of flabby businessmen sweating in their suits, their folding chairs squawking in protest as they retract their sausage-like limbs just enough to let me pass. I end up wedged between the largest of the men and the wall of church mailboxes. Instinctively, my eyes zero in on my old family slot, five from the left and three from the bottom. It's overflowing with envelopes. Sympathy cards for Abe, probably.

Sorry your dad died.

Sorry your wife left you.

Sorry your son is such a disappointment.

We hope for your sake it is true that the Good Lord never gives us more than we can bear, though in your case, Pastor Abe, we're starting to wonder.

I'm surprised to see Mayor Jake and not the old man take the stage to start the service. I've never known my father to miss a chance to deliver his patented eulogy and altar call combo. My uncle looks like a taller, tanner version of his younger brother, compensating for thinning hair with a smarmy smile that never leaves his face. The mayor's clearly in his element as he launches into some prepared remarks about Opa, pounding the pulpit and pausing for effect. He works the crowd with the ease of a career politician, which he is. The sound system whines in protest as his booming voice reverberates around the sanctuary. The guy in the AV booth moves frantically about, trying to adjust the levels. He might as well switch the sound board off. This is one man who has never needed a mic to make himself heard.

Mayor Jake has been in charge of Newfield's tiny town council since before I was born. He's the kind of person whose name and job title are almost always mentioned in the same breath. He's also the church moderator and chairs just about every board that exists in southeastern Manitoba. I remember him telling me once that he felt it was his heavenly calling to serve mankind through municipal politics, just as it was my father's duty to care for God's people as a pastor. Something about the way he said this made me want to become an anarchist.

Still, the man does have an impressive track record. He won his first election with ninety percent of the popular vote. As far as I know, he's been acclaimed ever since. It's not that he's so great at being mayor, but he meets the only requirements the job seems to have: consistent availability, a winning smile, and a beating heart, though the jury's still out on that last part. The status quo is rarely challenged in Mennoland, so at this point my uncle is pretty much mayor for life. Unless he comes out in support of Trudeau. Then he'd be run out of town right quick.

The mayor drones vaguely on about my grandfather's "servant heart" and "legacy of faithfulness" for a good twenty minutes while the muscles around my eyes grow twitchy from all the rolling. I can't believe this is the send-off we're giving Opa Willie. If I were up there right now, I'd be talking about the memories that have stuck with me over the years. The bags of licorice sticks he kept in his machine shop just for me. Red ones, because he knew I didn't like the black kind. About the only time I saw him cry, when the vet came to the farm and told him it was time to put down the last of the tiger brothers. He did it himself once Wonder World was closed for the day. Aunt Deb said he didn't eat for days afterwards.

Or I might have mentioned how even though he knew his only grandchild was a little out there, he loved me anyway. Opa Willie didn't care that I wasn't on a sports team, that I was a bookworm, that my best friend was a girl. While everyone else in my life was so busy trying to mould me into someone else's image, my grandfather delighted in who I was. He'd always find some excuse to get me out to the farm and put me on some special little job because he knew how much I liked being with him. If I made a mistake, he'd simply show me how to fix it, no guilt trip.

"Mistakes happen, kjint," he'd say, shrugging it off. "That's how you learn."

Opa had me over to the farmhouse for sleepovers almost every weekend growing up. He taught me to treat everyone as my neighbour and not sweat the small stuff. I can picture him perfectly, taking one of his many farm hats down off a nail in the shop and slipping it over his balding head. His favourite was the brown corduroy one with the John Deere logo on the front. There was a stain in the shape of his fingertips on one side from hands that were perpetually coated in dirt or grease or who knows what else.

When he was done for the day, he'd motion me over to his half-tonne. Tell me to hop in on the driver's side. Nervous but excited, I'd back us out and head for the fields. He'd rest a big, tanned arm out the open window, coaxing me along between sips of the coffee he kept in a dented plaid thermos.

"You just veer a little to the left now, jung, to miss that big stone. To the left. Well, that's alright. You'll miss it next time yet."

I avoided my whole family once I got kicked out of the church, thinking I could save myself some pain if I rejected them before they rejected me. I realize now how stupid that was. My grandfather was not a judgemental person. He was generous to a fault. All-forgiving. A patient player of the long game. In fact, I can't remember a single time Opa ever lost his temper around me, even with the snippiest customers at Wonder World. He was always just there, a gentle, reassuring constant in the background of my life when everything else was a mess.

I should have stopped by the farm to say goodbye when I left town. Sent him a birthday card with a twenty-dollar bill and a cartoon clipped out of the paper like he used to do for me. I could've at least called once I'd moved and told him about my new life in Halifax. The time it snowed for three days straight, and my roommates and I had to dig ourselves out with a dustpan and some pot lids because none of us owned a goddamn shovel. Swimming in the ocean with a joyful, overexcited Irish Setter who broke away from her owners at Rainbow Haven, my favourite beach. He would have laughed at my stories. He would have understood.

Mayor Jake finally finishes up The Eulogy of the Century and Abe takes his place. The crowd grows more animated, and a low murmur fills the room. Several people lift off their seats ever so slightly, craning their necks to get a better look at the stage.

A plump woman in front of me leans over to hiss in her companion's ear.

"He doesn't look sick to me."

"He's sick in the head, Anita, not the body. The elders called it a mental health leave, remember?"

"I still don't see why Pastor Abe needs three whole months off. A little fresh air and prayer, that's all he needs. Maybe he should go see your cousin."

"Which cousin?"

"The trajchtmoaka."

"Anita, what did I just tell you? Bones and brains are not the same thing!"

So my father hasn't been pastoring, or even attending, his church as of late. Did he not think I might find this out from someone else if he didn't tell me himself? Or perhaps that was his plan all along. He could count on this gossipy town to pass along his little life update without ever having to utter the word "depression" out loud.

Who are you without church Abe? How do you make sense of your world, and yourself, without it?

"There is a time for everything," the old man reads from the stage, "and a season for every activity under the heavens: a time to plant and a time to uproot, a time to embrace and a time to refrain from embracing, a time to be silent and a time to speak, a time to search and a time to give up, a time to weep and a time to laugh, a time to be born and a time to die."

I notice he skips over the bit about mourning and dancing. Even our own holy book can be a little too salacious for Mennos at times. Although he would call himself a biblical literalist, Abe isn't above a bit of scriptural revision every now and then when it suits his purposes. One Saturday night when I was fifteen, I got a bit too wasted at a bush party. When I got home, I couldn't get my key to line up with the lock and had to ring the doorbell. Abe didn't say anything when he let me in, but the next morning at church he preached a sermon insisting Jesus never turned H2O into merlot at Cana. Apparently the "best wine" all the wedding guests raved about was actually nutritious, delicious, and entirely unfermented grape juice.

The word of our Lord is brought to you this week by Welch's Grape Juice. Welch's: what would Jesus drink?

When his scripture reading is through, Abe immediately returns to his seat. Apparently, he is not to be trusted with any unscripted remarks today. A pinch-faced woman takes her place at the church piano and motions to the congregation. Everyone stands to sing a couple of hymns, standard stuff like "Great Is Thy Faithfulness" and "It Is Well With My Soul." We end with "Gott Ist Die Liebe" sung all in German, the only element of this service I could see Opa Willie approving. The song perks up the slumping old-timers, who jerk to attention en masse and belt out the words by heart while the rest of us fumble for the lyrics in our funeral bulletins. Still, we all, young and old, manage to slide into four-part harmony as smoothly as a canoe launched into a glassy lake. If there's one thing Mennos can come together on, it's a good old-fashioned hymn sing.

I do my best to join in, but my jaw quickly seizes up with a deep aching pain. My hands ball themselves into tight fists, strangling the words on the page.

The pianist is playing well enough, but it's not her limp, disinterested hands that should be filling this sanctuary with music. For years I was the star fixture on the NMC worship band. I didn't care about the content of the songs; I just wanted another opportunity to play the instrument I loved. On those Sunday mornings, I was happy as long as I was at the keys. Opa was happy too. He always told me I had "golden fingers."

It was my mother who inspired my early interest in the piano. Loreena and Abe met at a nearby bible college. He was studying theology while she was taking music. She was good enough that one of her professors arranged a big audition with the Winnipeg Symphony Orchestra for her. Abe got scared he was going to lose his girlfriend to greener pastures and made a hasty proposal. Loreena said yes, dropped out of school with a semester to go, and never went to that audition.

From what Opa told me, it sounds like she did her best to fit into her new role as pastor's wife and worship leader. Eventually, though, she had enough of this stifling microcosm and did exactly what Abe had once feared: she left. Her name might have become a four-letter word in Newfield after my parents' divorce, but members of the congregation would still fondly reminisce about her musical talents to me every so often. I realized as a kid that the piano could offer me the same way out as my mother, and music became my life. But I lost that spark after grad night, and unlike Loreena, I didn't impress any of my professors. I haven't touched a piano in years.

The mayor reclaims the pulpit to offer a benediction. My uncle is clearly running the show, and he seems to have decided that his youngest sibling Deb is best left off the speaker's list.

I can almost picture Opa Willie floating above the crowd, grumbling about the "big fuss" we're all making. He was a simple guy who never asked for anything except a slice of sour cream and raisin pie once a year for his birthday. He had plenty of money, but never spent it on himself. He never travelled, but seemed happiest on his porch swing, watching the sun set over his farm with a cup of coffee in hand. Especially if someone else was there to shoot the shit with.

I can't see my grandfather approving this grandstanding spectacle his eldest son has organized on his behalf, but the truth is this funeral isn't really for Opa. It's a chance for the mayor to reinforce the Funks' reputation as the ideal First Family of Newfield, despite the black sheep in our flock.

The pianist starts plunking out a depressing rendition of "'Tis So Sweet to Trust in Jesus" and the congregation rises for a final time. She drags the song out a good long while to give family members time to file out of the church first. Most of Opa's remaining cousins and siblings now live in Sunset Villa, Newfield's retirement home. They had to skip their afternoon nap to be here, so it takes a few minutes to crank-start the lot and get them rolling.

Eventually, the great cotton-haired cloud of witnesses inch down the aisle with an assortment of wheelchairs and walkers, coaxed along by a couple of aides in pastel scrubs. The home's most bossy and overbearing employee is hot on the group's heels, though thankfully for them she is off duty at the moment. Her spiky, asymmetrical bob, which is either blond with black highlights or black with blond highlights depending on how you look at it, shakes impatiently as she's forced to wait. It's always been easy to spot Aunt Gina. She hasn't changed her hairstyle or her opinions in forever. "The woman's got a finger in every pie," my aunt Deb used to say.

I've never understood why so many conservative church ladies get the queerest haircuts. Maybe it's because all of their hairdressers are gay and this is their secret way to get revenge on their most homophobic clients.

Then Fernando said unto Crispin, "Let us remake Regina Funk in our fabulous image, according to our fierce likeness. Let us charge her ninety bucks plus tax and tip for the privilege of the Basic Bitch Bob and Blowout package. And let her go forth into the world, proclaiming to all her friends that she hath been rendered Trendy by our hands. And let the fish of the sea and the birds of the sky and every living thing over all the earth laugh and rejoice that we hath used this hateful bigot to enrich our queer-ass selves."

I suppose I shouldn't be so tough on Gina. After all, Abe was always putting his pastoral duties above his parental ones, so she was often the one who drove me to music lessons or made me dinner or tucked me in at night. She and Jake weren't able to have any children of their own despite their fervent prayers and fertility treatments, so I tried to accept her meddling in my life as well-meaning kindness. But try as I might, I've just never really hit it off with the woman. Conversation didn't flow naturally between us like it did with Opa. I've always thought of her as the Martha to Deb's Mary. Perpetually striving for some future perfection, never able to enjoy the beauty of the present moment.

Mayor Jake glides along behind his wife. Unlike her, he's in no hurry to leave, and is more than happy to glad-hand and hobnob with the crowd. This church service might as well be a political rally to him.

Abe, meanwhile, is stuck at the front of the sanctuary with a burly man in an ill-fitting suit who strokes his unkempt beard with one hand while gesticulating wildly with the other. My father's face is frozen into a half smile. He nods politely along with each erratic chop of the other man's forearm, though he's obviously looking for a way out of the conversation.

I scan the congregation repeatedly but there's still no sign of Deb. Where could she be? There's no farm to look after now, and she and Opa had always been super close. I can't think of anywhere she'd rather be than his memorial service. Maybe she just didn't want to sit up front with the rest of the Funks. That I would understand.

I avoid shuffling off to the family-only interment at the cemetery on Main Street in the hopes I'll find Neth among the crowd of distant cousins and assorted spectators sticking around for the funeral reception. Several church ladies have already stationed themselves at opposite ends of the faspa table in the basement, swatting hungry children away from the food with tea towels and refilling a phalanx of rapidly emptying coffee urns. No one seems to care that it's at least thirty degrees outside.

I join the line more out of habit than need, but the last cup goes to the person ahead of me.

"Give us a couple minutes to brew some more," says a woman at the table, pouring me some tepid cloudy liquid before I can refuse.

Ah, the dreaded church juice. Bought in bulk at Costco and watered down to shit to make it last longer. The stuff tastes like lemon-scented laundry soap and turns your pee neon, but perhaps with two cups in hand I'll look like I have somewhere to be while I search for Neth. Anything to avoid the tedious circles of small talk expanding around the room.

"Is that for me?" someone wheezes. "That's very kind of you."

The person behind me waddles forward to claim my second cup of church juice. I recognize him as the same man who cornered Abe earlier. Oh God. It's too late. I've been sucked in.

One of the church ladies comes over and hands the man a paper plate piled high with hunks of cheddar, slices of rolled up ham, a raisin bun, and two pieces of rhubarb plautz. He thanks her profusely.

"Low blood sugar," he explains. "Would you mind? I'm afraid I'm a little shaky on my feet these days."

He holds out an elbow and has me guide him to a nearby table. He bows his head for a hasty grace before inviting me to join him, but I choose to remain standing while I plot my escape.

"Sorry, I think I see my friend over there. I should probably say hello."

"You look familiar," he says. "Were you at Mrs. Alvina Dueck's viewing in Kleefeld last Thursday?"

I shake my head.

"Must've been the service for Mr. Peter Pankratz of Blumenort then. Two weeks back?"

"Nope. Look, I'm afraid I really have to—"

I'm interrupted by a fit of coughing. The man appears to have inhaled his bun too quickly. He pulls a handkerchief from the pocket of his cheap polyester suit and horks up a lump of white mush dotted with flecks of raisin. As he does this, the desiccated remains of a half-eaten cookie crumble out of the handkerchief and onto the table. Spoils from his last spin around the Mennoland grief circuit, no doubt.

"That's better," he says with a chuckle. "Anyway, I'm sure I know you. What church do you attend?"

"I'm not from around here," I blurt out. "Just flew in for the funeral. Wanted to represent Trudy's side of the family."

I nod towards a slideshow of my grandfather's life playing on a loop behind us. A wedding photo of Willie and Trudy scrolls across the screen. I never knew my grandmother, but perhaps namedropping a woman who's been gone for fifty years might throw this man off the scent of who I really am.

"Ah, a budding genealogist, are we? Nice of you to come. My wife's niece was married to a cousin of the deceased, so of course

I had to pay my respects. Nothing's more important than family, is it? I'm sure Trudy and William are rejoicing at their heavenly reunion. My Lydia's been gone three years now and it sure is lonely at home without her. Who did you say your parents were again?"

"You know, I think the coffee's probably ready by now."

The man's eyes light up at the word "coffee." There it is. My ticket out of the Mennonite Game.

"Would you like me to go check on that for you?" I ask.

"Very kind," he murmurs as I slowly back away.

As soon as his attention is back on his plate, I bolt.

7

Neth isn't upstairs or anywhere outside that I can see. She wouldn't have left without saying hi, would she? I really don't want to bump into anyone who might recognize me and spread the word that Pastor Abe's pansexual problem child is back in town, so I opt to hide out in the men's bathroom while I wait for the rest of the Funks to return from the gravesite.

I sit in an empty stall while the bathroom door squeaks over and over, letting in a constant stream of urinal users. The place reeks of ammonia and potpourri, both scents doing their best to mask the shameful reality of our bodily functions. With nothing to do, I pull out my phone and open a dating app. My screen is instantly awash in a sea of body parts: legs, torsos, backs. Hunks of anonymous flesh, locations hidden and names withheld.

My own profile, with its clear face pic smiling up at me, seems totally out of place. I suppose that kind of transparency is a liability in the queer scene here, not a selling feature. But I'm done hiding. This is who I am boys. Take it or leave it. But, like, preferably take it. Please?

It's not entirely their fault of course. Queer or straight, everyone around here was raised on the same strict abstinence-only health class curriculum approved by the Southeastern School Division. It's no wonder so many of us developed hang ups about hookups as adults. I had more than my fair share of steamy encounters folded into a bathroom stall or a Honda Civic as a teenager, and I don't miss them. But that's only because I left Mennoland and saw what else was out there. If Abe hadn't caught me with Noah and outed me to the church, well then who knows? I might still be a closet case like the rest of the local queers on this app.

At least this Tetris of torsos does contain a number of pleasing specimens. A particularly hairy chest catches my eye and I scan through his profile. Unsurprisingly, he doesn't host. Another backseat blowjob, huh? Well, it could be worse.

I send him a friendly message and he responds almost immediately.

> Fuck off fatty.

The hairy chest disappears into the ether. Okay then. Guess I'm not his cup of masculinity.

Another user messages me. His picture is just a crotch shot zoomed in to highlight his bulging blue jeans and a steel belt buckle stamped with the image of a half-naked cowboy wrestling a bull to the ground. Subtle.

I open the notification. Alrighty then. That's a dick pic. And not a very good one either. Bro needs to learn about the benefits of backlighting.

He follows this gem up with a straightforward proposition.

> U down 2 suck???

You need to up your game my friend. Start with a compliment. Try to make me laugh maybe. A snapshot of your schlong does nothing for me. My generation grew up on LimeWire and MSN Search. I've had more than my fill of pixelated penises over the years. You know what really turns me on? A personality. But that's asking for too much these days, isn't it? Guess it's my turn to hit the block button.

The stall door rattles politely.

"Uh, hey, you alright in there? Don't mean to rush you or anything. We've just got a bit of a line up going here, is all."

Heat rushes to my cheeks as I hurry to my feet. At the last second, I stop short of sliding the lock open and turn back to flush the toilet. This will add an air of authenticity. Real men don't dawdle in the bathroom. They get shit done and move on.

When I open the door, a tall, sandy-haired guy about my age nearly bowls me over as he rushes inside. The fly on his formal jeans is already unzipped. He's cute, but also definitely my cousin somehow, so I swallow down a dirty joke, give my hands a cursory wash, and slip out the door.

I decide to text Neth a hey you here? After a minute, a response comes in, but it's not the one I'm hoping for.

> Vv sorry!! Babysitter cancelled last min and Connor was working…tried to bring thing 1 and thing 2 with me but they had a meltdown on the drive to the church about some spilled milk (literally) so I had to take them home and put on netflix until they turned into jellobrain babies. #parentinglikeapro amirite? XD lets hang soon tho k?? <3

Without a friend to lean on, my will to remain at the church evaporates.

Why isn't Abe back yet? Is he out there burying Opa by hand? I can just imagine my old man perspiring under the hot sun, his suit jacket cast off and tie askew, a smudge of dirt on his cheek where someone else might have wiped away a tear. It certainly wouldn't be an easy task to bury Opa without a backhoe considering our town is built on Manitoba gumbo, a rich dark soil that clumps together like wet clay. It would make sense for Abe to say goodbye with an act of physical exertion. As hard as it is to shovel dirt over your father's grave, it's still easier than trying to say "I love you" out loud.

Why did I ever think it would be a good idea for me to come back here? To this place, among these people. None of this is

mine anymore. Not this church, this faith, this town. I'm sorry
Opa, but I've got to go.

Of course, Abe reaches the other side of the main doors just
as I'm about to make my escape.

"Leaving?" the old man asks.

I give a curt nod.

"Oh." He has a nervous look in his eyes. "We're about to start
the lunch."

"I'm sorry, but I just can't—"

There's a strangled squeak behind Abe's left shoulder, like someone choking on a chicken bone. My eyes water as I'm enveloped by
a cloud of hairspray and perfume. Gina and Jake materialize just
behind Abe. My aunt masks her initial shock with a thin-lipped
smile that does not reach her eyes.

"Isaac *Funk*. As I *live* and *breathe*!" she says.

"Nephew!" my uncle exclaims with false cheer. "What a pleasant
surprise!"

Gina raps my old man on the knuckles. *"Abraham,* you silly
man, why didn't you *tell* us you'd managed to track him down?"

Jake clamps a hand on Abe's shoulder. "Yes, brother, how did
you do it?"

"I called the university," Abe says, addressing his shoes. "I
explained the situation and a young lady in the Registrar's Office
was kind enough to help me out."

I was wondering how he'd managed to get hold of my Nova
Scotia number. I didn't think anyone in Newfield had it. I've got
to remember not to cut Dalhousie any cheques if I ever become
rich and famous.

Gina's bony fingers and chunky rings dig into my arms as she
reels me in and plants a parched kiss on my cheek. "It's so *good*
to see you, young man. You're a *ray* of sunshine on this *dark* day.
If I'd only *known* you were coming, I'd have made *sure* you sat
up front with the rest of the family."

Okay, who are you and what have you done with my aunt?

She couldn't even look at me outside the elders meeting with Noah, just passed along a note before bursting into tears and rushing away. It was an article from some so-called family values website entitled "The Many Health Risks of the Homosexual Lifestyle." At the top of the printout, she'd hastily scrawled half a bible verse.

> *Isaac, always remember: For the wages of sin is death, but the gift of God is eternal life in Christ Jesus our Lord.*
> *Love, Auntie Regina*

As for my uncle Jake, he thoroughly enjoyed using his role as church moderator to sit in judgement of me. I thought he was going to have a full-on powergasm as he explained how much it "pained" him to have this "delicate conversation," but that, regrettably, my "egregious lapse of judgement" had "forced his hand." It was like the world's worst episode of *Law & Order*. I half expected him to pull out a doll and ask Noah to show the members of the jury where I'd touched him.

Why are these two suddenly playing nice with me?

"Surely you'll join us for faspa and freiwilliges?" the mayor asks. "There's so much to talk about."

Gina gives her hair an aggressive coiffing with a flick of her manicured fingernails and launches into frenzied planning for a big family dinner. When she finally finishes, it takes me a moment to resurface and realize that everyone is waiting for me to speak.

"I have to go," I say, the words catching on the back of my throat.

"*Certainly*, dear. You must be so tired after travelling *all this way*. You go rest up and we'll visit later. When did your flight get in? Did you have an aisle seat?"

"No Auntie, I mean I have to leave town. It was a mistake to come back. This isn't my home anymore."

I look to my old man, watching for any sign of protest or push back that might encourage me to stay. His lips part ever so slightly, but no sound escapes. Instead, it's my uncle who speaks.

"Well, that's a real shame, but if your mind's made up then we won't try to stop you."

I ignore him and keep my eyes on Abe. "Aunt Deb can call me if there are papers to sign or whatever for the will. Okay?"

"Absolutely," the mayor answers, stepping between us. "You can count on us. Take care of yourself, Nephew. Now, who's hungry?"

Jake and Gina steer my father down the stairs towards the reception. I don't know why I wait for him to look back. I should know better by now.

8

I'm trying to remember whether my thumb should be tilted to the side or straight up to indicate I'm looking for a ride. Not a single vehicle has slowed down for me since I stuffed all my clothes and the half-empty box of wine into my bag back at Abe's place and started walking until Main Street became the highway. Does anyone even hitchhike anymore?

I don't know what to do or where to go beyond heading in the general direction of St. Mary's Road. The oxfords are pinching my feet, but at least the angry knot of tension between my shoulder blades seems to relax a bit more with each step I take away from Newfield. I've traded the blazer and button-up for a hot pink tank top with arm holes ripped down almost to my hips. The remaining material keeps riding up over my love handles as I walk. The chinos I ditched for a pair of frayed denim shorts cut off at a length most Newfielders would find shocking on a person of any age or gender. I'm sure my look probably isn't helping my chances to get a ride into Winnipeg, but it's hotter than hell under the prairie sun. Since all of NMC believes I lost any sense of moral decency years ago, I might as well stay cool and give them one last show at the same time.

A half hour into my walk I pass the sign for Opa's place, a giant sheet of plyboard that used to display a folksy painting of my grandfather holding hands with a tiger, a turtle, and a duck under a long red banner saying *Welcome to Wonder World* in large white block letters. I missed seeing the farm on my ride into town with Abe yesterday, but now, up close, the place is really showing its age.

The paint on the sign has mostly faded. Opa's face is too faint to make out, and all the animals are missing limbs or tails. The fence posts of the property are greyed with age and poke out of the ground like a row of crooked teeth. There is no movement within their enclosure, which is for the best since I doubt the rusty barbed wire strung between the road and three-storey farmhouse could hold back a sudden gust of wind, let alone the giraffe who used to live in this field.

The house itself is dark and unkempt. Several shutters are missing from the windows and a number of shingles have detached from the roof and lie strewn about the yard. There are dozens of potholes in the large patch of gravel to the south of the house where Opa used to station me in the summer. I earned five dollars a day helping visitors park there. I thought I was the most important person in the world, wearing my orange reflective vest and waving cars to the left or right.

A tear rolls down my sunburnt cheek. Opa took such pride in Wonder World. I don't think I ever saw him here without a paint brush or a hammer or a tape measure in hand. Over the years he sold most of his land to care for the animals and bring in new attractions that would entice more visitors. It must have broken his heart to see this place become so rundown once he moved into town. And now he'll never have the chance to fix it up again.

The low rumbling of something big coming along the highway interrupts the moment. I throw my thumb up half-heartedly and to my surprise a semi slows down and pulls onto the shoulder behind me. Success!

White feathers drift out of slats in the truck's metal trailer, falling to the ground like the first October snowfall. Must be hauling poultry. A gust of wind brings a whiff of bird shit my way, confirming my suspicions. My nose wrinkles at the stench.

"Hey there, bud. Need a ride?"

It's hard to hear the driver over his idling engine and the twang of a country song. He smiles with nicotine-stained teeth and beckons me closer. The man is greasy-haired and gangly, and I can't tell whether he's a rough looking thirty-something or a half-decent forty-something.

"That's okay. I don't have far to go."

Not to stereotype or anything, but if I worked for a casting agency, I'd hire this guy for my next slasher flick in a heartbeat. Something about him just gives off Your Friendly Neighbourhood Serial Killer vibes. Probably best to pass on the trucker's offer. I'm sure someone else will come along.

"Really? Where you headed?"

I try to answer, but this time my tongue stays glued to the roof of my mouth. Now that I've stopped moving, the cumulative effects of this long walk under a scorching sun are starting to catch up to me. My brain seems to have turned into scrambled eggs. I stand there, swaying slightly, and stare up at the man with incomprehension.

"Winnipeg?" he finally suggests.

I find myself nodding in agreement.

"Well, you won't get there anytime soon on foot, bud. It's no trouble for me, really. Just taking a load of turkeys to Transcona for processing. But it's up to you."

Okay, so he's literally on his way to a slaughterhouse. That's not creepy at all.

I scan the road for any other ride options, but it's totally deserted. This guy looks short. Scrawny. I could take him if I needed to, right? And really, who else around here is going to stop for a chubby queer in a pair of DIY Daisy Dukes?

The city's as good a place as any to hide out while I plot my next move. Maybe this guy could drop me off at a mall or something. Just as long as it isn't St. Vital. That place is always crawling with Newfielders swapping sale prices and gossip at the food court.

"Um, yeah. I guess I will take a ride if you don't mind. Thanks."

"My pleasure, bud! Hop in."

The trucker leans over to open his passenger side door for me. I take my phone out while he isn't looking and snap a discreet photo of his licence plate, just in case. I swing my bag up and step into the cab. Something crunches under my ass as I plunk down onto the seat. I reach down and find a half-empty bag of ketchup chips. There are candy wrappers and fast-food packaging scattered all throughout the truck. I can't help but make a face.

"Sorry about the mess."

He reaches over and I almost flinch before realizing he's just turning down the radio.

"I'm a bit of a slob I know," he continues. "But hey, a free ride's a free ride, eh? I'm Elmer by the way."

"Isaac."

"Nice to meet you."

We shake hands, awkwardly. His is warm and soft like bread dough. We touch for a second longer than I mean to before Elmer lets go and pulls back out onto the road.

"So, Isaac. Where you coming from?"

"Newfield."

The town recedes behind us in the truck's side mirror.

"Going on a little trip or something?" Elmer asks, gesturing to my backpack.

"Yep."

The trucker waits for more of an answer, but I don't offer one. He works a piece of food out from between his teeth with a thick fingernail, then grins into the rear-view to make sure it's gone.

"You're not really a talkative fella, are you Isaac?"

I shrug, keeping my eyes on the world outside my window.

"Sorry, it's just been a long day."

"Hey, I hear ya, bud. No worries. We don't have to talk. Plenty of other ways to spend our time."

Something about the way he says this makes me shrink back

into my seat ever so slightly. The truck purrs into a lower gear as we approach the junction with St. Mary's Road.

"So, you got a girlfriend, Isaac? If you don't mind me asking?"

"Nope."

"Nope to the question or the girlfriend?"

"Both."

"A boyfriend maybe?" Elmer presses.

A prickling sensation travels up the back of my spine. I eye the trucker cautiously. He's got a playful smirk on his face, and his hands are resting on the steering wheel with a casual ease. Is he trying to stir shit up or is he genuinely curious?

"I am unattached at the moment," I finally say.

Elmer furrows his brow. "Really? Attractive fella like you? I would've thought you'd have been taken off the market long ago."

"Yeah, who wouldn't want a piece of this?" I joke, patting the prominent belly beneath my sweat-soaked shirt.

"Sorry, don't mean to make you uncomfortable." Elmer shifts in his seat, finally breaking eye contact. "I'll try and keep my big mouth shut."

Ugh, poor guy. He's probably just a lonely closet case looking for some sympathy. A road sign tells me it's ten kilometres to St. Stache and thirty to Winnipeg. We've got some time yet. And he is giving me a free ride. The least I could do is show a little interest in this conversation.

I tilt a couple of vents in my direction until the AC hits me just right, and give my grubby guardian angel a second chance.

"What about you Elmer? You seeing anybody at the moment?"

The trucker blushes to the back of his neck. "Nope, not me, bud. It's tough being on the road all the time, you feel me? Hard to meet people. Or keep 'em around."

"I get that. How long you been trucking?"

"Eighteen years."

"And what's the longest trip you've done?"

"Six thousand klicks there and back."

"Really? Wow!" I add a hint of wonder to my voice and Elmer flushes a few shades deeper. Okay, bud. I see you. "Across country or—?"

"Saskatoon to Chihuahua, actually. A friend of mine was moving down there. He had family in Mexico. Mennonites. I thought they were all prairie people, but I guess there's a whole bunch of them down there in some of those Spanish countries too."

The trucker's voice pitches higher as the words tumble out. He's obviously pleased to have someone take an interest in him, even if it's feigned.

"Anyway, I figured he might want to pay for a real moving company, but he said he wanted to go with someone he could trust. Paid in cash too, which was real nice. Tax man takes too much, if you ask me."

"Did you get to swim in the ocean? I bet there were some great beaches down there."

"Nope, it's basically a straight line down through the Midwestern States actually. Saskatchewan, Montana, Wyoming, Colorado, New Mexico, Old Mexico." He waits a beat, then looks over. "Get it?"

I purse my lips in bemusement.

"Chihuahua's actually completely landlocked," he continues. "So I never seen the ocean."

Saw. Saw the ocean.

He's looking at me, expecting a response, but my mind has gone blank. What were we just talking about? Right. His friend. The words come out of my mouth before I have a chance to think them through.

"I'm Mennonite too, actually."

Elmer's tongue flicks out from between his teeth like he's tasting my words. "That so?" he says, wetting the cracked skin of his lips. "Figured you might be with that bible name of yours."

"You can blame my dad for that one."

"He religious?"

"Oh yeah. A pastor even."

Do I have heat stroke? This guy doesn't deserve my life story. It's time to take the spotlight off me. "You don't happen to have any water, do you?" I ask.

The trucker perks up, eager to please.

"Sure do, bud! There's a mini fridge in the back. Help yourself to anything you see."

Glancing behind us, I'm amazed to find his bed is relatively clean. There's not a dirty gitch or crusty sock in sight. God, I really am a judgey person, aren't I? The guy's just trying to be friendly.

Elmer notices my hesitation. "Don't worry. I'll keep 'er nice and steady for ya."

"Thanks."

I unbuckle my seatbelt and crawl into the back of the cab, trying not to think about this man keeping anything nice and steady. Truth be told, I am pretty hungry. I was counting on filling up at faspa, but those church ladies kept a fierce watch on their Saran-wrapped goodies the whole time I was there.

Elmer's little fridge is full of bottled water and those packaged sandwiches they sell in gas stations. I opt for a ham and cheese that's only slightly grey around the edges. Standing up, something catches my eye. The shirtless image of an airbrushed hunk peaks out from under the trucker's pillow alongside a cylindrical object with pink puckering lips. Well, there. Who needs a sock when you've got your very own Fleshlight? Elmer, you poor lonely horndog. I could make a joke, but it's probably best to ignore what I've found. I don't want to embarrass the guy when he's being so nice.

"Thanks for the—"

Turning back to face the front seats, I spot a substantial bulge in the trucker's jeans. From this vantage point, I can make out the image on his chunky silver belt buckle as well, a muscly guy wrapped around a snorting bull.

Wait a second. I've seen this before. But where?

Oh fuck. I'm hitching a ride with U down 2 suck guy.

"You say something?"

My eyes dart away from Elmer's crotch as he glances back at me. "Huh?"

"Thanks for what?"

"Oh! The sandwich."

I leave the water and hop back over my bag, careful not to brush against the other man's leg as I take my seat.

"You're easily distracted, huh?" There's a hungry look on the trucker's face.

"Sorry?"

"Just joking with ya, bud. No worries."

This is getting weird. Well, weirder. I slide a hand into my pocket and take out my phone, keeping it covered on my lap.

"You gone quiet on me again Isaac."

"Sorry," I mumble.

"It's fine. We'll get you out of your shell yet." He throws me a sidelong glance. "Speaking of which, you wearing anything under those sexy little cut-offs of yours or what?"

"Elmer—"

"You shouldn't have blocked me earlier. I was just trying to be friendly. You gotta give people a chance sometimes, bud."

Damn it, I knew I should have ditched the face pic on that app! My stomach and heart lurch in opposite directions, scrambling to escape the cab. "Look, I—"

"You know, I gave you the benefit of the doubt this afternoon. Most people don't stop for hitchhikers no more. But I did you a solid cause I'm a nice guy. A nice guy who happens to be real into bears."

"I'm sorry Elmer, but I think there's been some kind of misunderstanding here."

Keep your cool. He isn't the first asswipe you've come across. There's a way out of this. Just think.

"Stop apologizing! It's annoying as fuck."

"Okay, but can you please calm down?"

"Don't tell me what to do."

I swallow down another "sorry" and quietly set the sandwich down between us, hoping he doesn't notice the shake in my hand.

"Look, I appreciate the ride, but I don't think we're interested in the same thing here."

"Aren't we?"

Elmer takes a hand off the wheel and lets it rest on my knee. Slowly, he starts to inch higher up my thigh, sliding his clammy fingers over the raised hairs on my leg. Past the fringed edge of my shorts. Towards the centre of my lap.

There's a road sign up ahead. *Bienvenue à Saint-Eustache-sur-la-Rivière.* I put my hand over top of the trucker's. Press down gently but firmly to stop his advance.

"No, Elmer."

"Come on, bud. Don't be like that. Give me a chance."

His fingers dig deeper into my thigh. We reach the outskirts of St. Stache and slow down to town speed. I could make a jump now if I have to, though I might break an arm in the process. I peel his hand off my leg and reach down towards the strap of my backpack.

"I'd like to get out here. Can you please pull over?"

The speedometer doesn't waver.

"I said stop the truck!"

"I heard you the first time, faggot!" Elmer says, glaring out the windshield. "But I'm not some goddamned taxi service. You get out when I say you can get out."

I flip my phone over in my lap and start to type out a message with one thumb.

"I'm the one who stopped for you," he continues. "I'm a nice fucking guy. You owe me."

I take a deep breath. Grip my phone tighter. Then I soften my face and twist towards him in my seat, laying a hand on his tensed forearm.

"Okay. You're right. Let's work something out."

"Really?"

The trucker turns to me in triumph. I wait until just the right moment to hit the flash and capture his smarmy face. I send the text before he can stop me.

"Here's the deal," I say, doing my best to keep my voice steady. "That was my friend I just texted. She has your face and your licence plate, and she's going to dial 911 if she doesn't hear from me in two minutes. Now pull over."

Elmer slams on the brakes. Someone behind him honks. He looks scared now.

"You called the fucking cops on me?"

"Not yet, but my friend will. Now am I free to go?"

We both glance at my phone.

"Minute and a half," I say.

"Look. I don't want any trouble. No one knows that I'm … that way."

His voice has pitched into a panicked whine. Every muscle in my body is taut, ready to spring. Please let this work. Please.

"I get it," I say, "and I don't want any trouble either. So just let me out and I'll be on my way. Okay?"

At first, I think he might punch me, but then he hangs his head. We lurch to a stop, kissing the curb.

My pulse pounds in my fingertips as I haul on my bag and reach for the door handle. I wait until I'm all the way out before speaking again.

"Oh, and Elmer? It would be super easy for me to share my story and your photo with a bunch of people online, so I wouldn't pick up any more hitchhikers if I were you. Are we clear on that?"

An angry flush of blood mottles his cheeks, but he nods in agreement.

"Great! Then have a nice life, you sad motherfucker."

I slam the door and the trucker takes off, the load of turkeys gobbling in indignation as he hauls them off to the poultry plant.

9

A shudder passes through my body as I stand there, dazed and blinking in the late-afternoon sun. The Timmy's across the road shimmers in the heat like a mirage. It sure would be nice to sit down there and catch my breath. Maybe grab a bagel and an iced capp while I figure out what to do next.

I try to take a step forward, but my legs quiver and buckle and I crumple to the ground.

Shit, I'm going to be sick.

No. I'm okay. Nothing happened! Not really. Right?

I grab onto a thick rusty signpost for support and pull myself back up. Looking at it, I realize where exactly I am and can't decide whether to blubber or laugh. How many times have Neth and I stood in this gravel lot under this buzzy, flickering sign, waiting for her cousin to come back out with our beer? That long, low building behind me with its peeling wooden siding and corrugated roof painted a cheap shade of green to cover the rust is the source of some of the best nights of my teenage years. Who would've guessed that jerk would drop me off right in front of the Rouge, St. Stache's legendary dive bar? I've never actually been inside myself. Wasn't legal yet the last time I lived here. I doubt this place would have carded us, but Neth and I didn't want to risk getting banned from our closest source of booze back in the day.

Though it's still fairly early, the bar's neon *Open/Ouvert* sign is already lit. There's a cracked marquee over the front door advertising *WINGS NIGHT AND TRIVIA EVERY MONDAY.* A few vehicles are parked outside, including an old half-tonne that reminds me of Opa's. I'll take that as a good omen. Guess it's time to pull back the curtain on the Rouge.

I send a follow up text to Neth before heading in.

> sorry to bother you i was actually able to find your store hours online

After hitting send, I start to type out another message to her.

> you won't believe what just

No. Don't freak her out. She's got enough on her plate.

> missed you at opa's

Once again I tap the delete button until the words disappear, then put my phone away. Try not to think about the fact there isn't anyone in my contacts I would have actually messaged about the trucker. I'm glad he didn't call my bluff.

Inside the Rouge, it takes my eyes a second to adjust to the bar's dim, windowless interior. Sunlight streams in behind me from the open door, illuminating every dancing dust particle in the air for the briefest moment before everything is plunged back into a moody twilight.

The place is mostly empty aside from a rowdy group in the corner who've pushed a few tables together. They're having a great time, laughing and carrying on. Also drinking. A lot. The empties are already piling up around them and it's not even five o'clock yet. I wonder what time they started.

A woman detaches herself from the group and heads towards the bar. She has a familiar gait, quick and confident. I remember struggling to keep up to it when I was a kid. What are the chances?

I move to the left and block her path.

"Hey."

She stops mid-stride and stares.

"Isaac?"

The woman reaches out a hand. Pulls back, uncertain. Then she's wrapping me in a spine-cracking bear hug. So much for the Funk family not being huggers!

"Good. To. See you. Too. Deb," I wheeze.

My aunt doesn't appear to have changed much in the last ten years. Same blue jeans and boots, salt and pepper hair cropped close and swept back out of her eyes, a pack of smokes in the front pocket of her flannel shirt. She releases me from her strong grip with a laugh. Reinflating is a bit painful, but what's a couple of bruised ribs after a greeting like that? My heart is pulsing with a strange sensation I can't quite name. One of my relatives seems genuinely happy to see me.

"What's with the bag?" Deb asks, giving my backpack a playful tug. "You're not skipping town again, are you?"

"Actually, yes," I say, looking away. "Maybe? I think. It's a long story."

My aunt frowns. "Well, why don't we grab a couple of cold ones and catch up first? I've been meaning to reach out anyway, what with the will and all. Unless you're in a hurry?"

"No, drinks sound great!" I say, smacking my hands together. Then I remember how broke I am.

"If you're buying?"

Deb laughs.

"Sure, kid. You got it."

Growing up, there were only three acceptable reasons to leave town:
1. Going to bible camp in the Whiteshell
2. Christmas shopping at Winnipeg's last surviving Christian bookstore
3. Lining up for the two-for-one farmer sausage sale at the good butcher in Steinbach

It's possible to live your whole life in Newfield without setting foot in St. Stache, even though it's only fifteen minutes away by car. Unless you're in need of a hospital, bar, or worse, a Catholic priest, most Mennos see no need to mix with our French neighbours. The elders at NMC warned us as teens not to visit St. Stache lest we get "sucked into worldliness." After a few beer runs to the Rouge with Neth and her cousin though, I realized what they were really saying was "please don't go, you might realize how much better life is out there."

It was amazing to visit a place where life didn't revolve around the church. People in St. Stache still go to mass at the RC church with the two steeples on the edge of the Red. And they take great pride in keeping the building's silvery metal roof and white plaster walls gleaming year-round. But the beating heart of the community during moments of both celebration and tragedy is unquestionably La Rivière Rouge Air-Conditioned Motor Inn, Beer Store, VLTs, and Licensed Bar and Grill. People simply call it the Rouge, just as they shorten the town's Christian name, Saint-Eustache-sur-la-Rivière, to something a little more manageable. This is a bare bones, no-nonsense kind of town, where everything gets boiled down to its essence like sap into syrup. There's probably still a couple of dingy rooms for rent somewhere in the back, but I'd sooner take a swig from the dusty bottle of house red that is permanently fused to the top shelf of the bar than pay somebody actual money to sleep on those crunchy sheets. Still, it's not a bad place to spend some of your night. The booze is cheap and the people are friendly. Everyone's mingling side-by-side, forgetting the cares of the world together one drink at a time.

When Deb brings me over to her party, I'm surprised to find that introductions are largely unnecessary. Most of the people gathered around these tables are former employees of Wonder World.

"Hey, is that Josephine?" I ask, pointing out a figure in a *Keepin' It Riel* t-shirt and vintage jean jacket. "She used to come up with the coolest corn maze designs!"

"Actually, they go by Jo now," Deb says.

"Oh, cool! Thanks for letting me know. What're they up to these days? I heard Wonder World closed down a while back."

"Jo, uh, owns a landscaping business." Deb glances towards the bar and tucks the wayward edge of her shirt back in place with a quick hook of her finger. "Would you excuse me just a minute? Next round's on me and I don't want to keep folks waiting."

Before I can react to Deb's abrupt departure, I'm beckoned over to a friendly table. A spindle-back chair is kicked out for me. My shoes stick to the floor with each step towards it. The centre of the seat gleams, dark varnish worn away by thousands of denim-clad derrieres. It's the only polished thing in this place.

"Isaac, you came! That's made your aunt's day for sure."

"Good to see you again, Jo."

They turn to their companion. "Chantal, this is Deb's nephew. He's been out East the past decade. Used to follow me around his grandpa's farm like a lost puppy."

"What can I say? You had all the cool toys," I joke. "Woodchipper, forklift, that cranky old weed-whacker."

"Don't remind me about that hunk of junk! Nearly tore my damn arm off trying to get it started every day."

"East as in East Coast?" Chantal asks.

"Yep. I went to Dal for music."

As soon as she hears this, Chantal is eager to tell me about her days fronting PHLEGMBOT, an all-trans punk band.

"Our very first sold-out show was in Halifax. Some place with rusty bike tires and mannequin parts nailed to the ceiling. It was wild! Bluenosers can frigging drink!"

"Yeah, I had some good parties at uni for sure. But what about you folks? This place is packed. Trivia night must be a big draw around here."

Chantal and Jo share a glance.

"Actually, trivia got cancelled," Chantal says. "Not that anybody's complaining. My sweet Jo here wins every damn round."

Jo offers a wry smile and leans back in their chair. "What can I say? Landscapers can get through a lot of podcasts in a ten-hour day. But, no, we're actually here for Willie. Kind of a Triple L wake, I guess. Sorry Isaac, thought that's why you showed up."

"What's Triple L?"

Jo scratches at their neck, chair thunking back down to the ground. "Oh geez, that's—well. Started as a book club back in the eighties, Deb's idea. Most of us were hanging out after our shifts at the farm anyway, so she decided to make it official. We called ourselves the Lesbian Literary and Libations Society, but over time that got shortened to Triple L. Two-Spirit, bi, trans, everybody's welcome. We kind of have Willie to thank for bringing us all together, I guess. Not all of us worked at Wonder World, but many did. There weren't a lot of safe employers back in the day for people like us, hey?"

"We have poker nights, hiking trips, stuff all over the southeast," Chantal adds. "Not all of us fit into big city life. Don't want to, either. Take Bev and Dorothea over there. They met on the plant floor of Froese Printers forty years ago, and they've been together ever since. Only time they've been to Winnipeg that I can think of was Dorothea's cataract surgery last fall. Small-town living is what we know. Triple L has become our community. We're not going anywhere."

"And the Rouge is really okay with you folks hanging out here?" I ask, still not quite able to believe what I'm hearing.

Chantal laughs. "Of course! The owner, Sandy, actually introduced me to Triple L when PHLEGMBOT broke up and I moved back home to St. Stache. She lets us use the kitchen here to can salsa and jam every fall. Sandy's wife Maureen is the minister at Newfield United, actually. There's a bunch of us in the choir and Maureen even convinced me to join their weekly quilting bee. The seniors there are all so sweet. Never thought I'd have so much fun in a church!"

I grip the tacky edge of the table for a moment, feeling off balance. Seems like someone's hooked my head up to a helium tank. It's going to detach and float away if I take any more of this in.

"Would you excuse me for a second? Just want to check in with my aunt."

"For sure," Jo says, offering to watch my bag.

I bump past several more acquaintances on my way to the bar ranging in age from thirty to seventy. Pearl was a few grades above me at school and she worked in Opa's petting zoo during the summer while going to college. She was well-known and well-liked by her fellow students, having served as volleyball captain, drama club lead, and student council president. These days she's rocking an undercut and a large triangle tattoo on one forearm.

There's a lusciously bearded man beside Pearl whose name I've forgotten, though my gut still flutters at the memory of him passing by with a push mower, a damp cotton shirt clinging to his ample belly in all the right places. I wanted to lick the sweat right off his bald head. He sees me checking him out and winks back. It's a good thing I've reached the bar. Gives me something to hold onto when the room goes wobbly.

"What can I get you?"

I take a breath and Sandy comes into focus, a full sleeve of tattoos on both arms and thick black hair curling around her face like smoke.

"Beer. Biggest glass you got. Please."

"This is the Rouge, hun," Sandy says. "We sell wings by the pound, and beer by the can or case. Best I can do is a tallboy."

I nod in agreement.

"Sorry," I say, remembering my empty wallet, "this is going to sound so dumb, but Deb is actually picking up my tab tonight. If that's okay?"

"No worries. She mentioned. Welcome back, by the way."

"Thanks. Did you happen to see where my aunt went?"

A bell dings in the kitchen. Sandy deftly retrieves a basket of wings with one hand while sliding me a drink with the other and jerking her chin towards the rear exit.

"Out back. Taking a smoke break. A long one. Go easy on her, eh? She wasn't expecting to see any family tonight."

"Will do. Thanks for the drink. And the advice."

I have so many questions:

1. How did I not notice that most of Wonder World's staff were queer?
2. Why is this the first I'm hearing of the very badass and super rad Triple L Society?
3. Most importantly, when was somebody going to tell me I have a gay aunt???

I guess I must have kept my gaydar way at the back of my bedroom closet when I was a kid, along with the Barbie doll I stole from Tina Warkentin's backpack in kindergarten and the Sears Wish Books I hauled out of the recycling every Boxing Day so I could peruse the underwear models—both briefs and panties—after my old man went to bed. Even at five or six, I knew how broken and sinful I was. That I couldn't tell anyone about my desires. Abe never needed to preach a homophobic sermon for me to internalize the Fear the Queer message. From Adam and Eve to the two-by-two pairings on Noah's ark, everyone in Mennoland knew the whole wide world was ostensibly descended from neat, nuclear, heteronormative, monogamous, bible-believing unions of husbands and wives forever and ever, amen goddammit. Of course I had the internet, so I knew I wasn't the only queer kid in existence. I just figured we could only be ourselves in Toronto or New York. We weren't supposed to have hometowns, just places we survived while we plotted our escape. And yet, this whole time, the Triple L folks were here making a life for themselves in Mennoland. Who would that scared little kid be now if he had known?

The floorboards creak and sag under my weight as I step out onto the Rouge's back deck. Tattered plastic sheets stapled to the posts stand in for windows, billowing like sails in the summer breeze. Deb is alone, sitting at a dirty glass patio table with an ashtray and a couple of empties.

I take a seat beside her. She sniffs. Runs a hand across her face to wipe away the tears.

"You smoke, kid?"

I think of Noah and his shaking hands.

"Not since high school."

"Good. You shouldn't. It's a filthy habit."

Then the smoke from her cigarette drifts my way and an old longing fills me. I cave instantly and bum a dart. Deb passes me her lighter without judgement, a classy chrome Zippo finely engraved with two tigers.

A pleasant, tingling rush pulses through my limbs as the nicotine sinks its pointed teeth into every inch of me. God. I'd forgotten how good it can feel to just chill for half a fucking second and suck some calming poison into your lungs.

We puff away in companionable silence for a while before I speak again.

"Well, this is hands down the best Mennonite wake I've ever been to. Wasn't aware we had that option."

Deb offers a weary smile.

"I've learned to pick my battles when it comes to Jake," she says, "and my heart just wasn't in this one. I haven't stepped foot in NMC for thirty years. I didn't want to be a spectacle, so I let my brother have his big to-do and decided to honour Dad in my own way."

"If it helps, you didn't miss much," I say. "I think Opa would have wanted something a lot smaller."

"Maureen offered to do something for me at Newfield United, but competing services just felt petty, you know? I'm glad Jo convinced me to do tonight instead. It's still hard, but at least I'm not alone."

"Wait, back up. Do you go to church?" I can't hide the shock in my voice.

Deb nods. "Every now and then since I got back from Saskatoon. Maureen's a good friend. She's counselled me through some rough times."

All this time I assumed Deb wasn't religious just because she didn't go to Abe's church. I guess my old man wouldn't exactly broadcast the fact that his sister attended such a progressive place of worship. I mean, people in Mennoland believe you can pray the gay away, that even atheists can be reasoned with. But once you've gone over to the United Church? Your spot in hell is all but guaranteed alongside feminists, pro-choicers, and anyone who's ever voted NDP.

I'm sure Opa was just happy to see his daughter find a place in town where she felt comfortable and accepted. Their bond was strong from day one, when Oma Trudy died giving birth to Deb. Some other father might have resented his daughter for this, but instead she became his reason to get out of bed in the morning. If he let the grief swallow him, his children would be down two parents instead of just one. Willie wasn't going to let that happen.

"I was the first man in Newfield to change a diaper!" he'd boast as we drove to some errand together. "The church ladies were always finding some excuse to drop by and check up on the children, make sure the freezer was well stocked. They thought a poor widower like me couldn't raise a family and run a business all on my own. But I managed just fine!

"Sure I'd prick Deb with the safety pin half the time, and dinner was eggs or beans on toast most nights, but we were alright. That was my promise to Trudy when she passed. I told her I'd always take care of our children, especially the little one she gave her life to bring into this world."

It was a hard go initially, trying to balance life as a farmer and single father. Opa began to think about selling his land and moving into town. But then one of his sisters sent him a postcard from a holiday to Alberta, where she'd visited a game farm. Animals were a lot of work, but at least he wouldn't have to spend so much time in the fields. He decided to give it a go, and Wonder World was born.

This openness to change was rare in Mennoland, and luckily for Deb it extended to Opa's parenting style too. His youngest child had always loved caring for animals and dreamed of one day becoming a vet. Most women in Newfield learn to give up on such lofty ambitions long before they graduate from the K-12 school on Main Street, but Willie encouraged his daughter every step of the way. She graduated top of her high school class, aced her pre-reqs at the U of M, and was quickly admitted to the Western College of Veterinary Medicine in Saskatoon. Before she could finish her studies, however, Opa had a heart attack. He was alone, and instead of calling his sons for help, he decided to take himself to the hospital in St. Stache. The doctors said the blockage was so bad he was lucky to survive the drive, let alone the operation that followed. Deb dropped everything to get him back on his feet, then stuck around to help him manage Wonder World. Like the rest of the family, I didn't interact with her much as a kid, but I have a general sense of her as a quiet, kind-hearted, and endlessly reliable presence on the farm. "I may be the face of this place," Opa would often say, "but Deb is the hands and feet!"

"I'm glad you have Maureen, and all the Triple L folks," I tell her. "I always thought I'd have to leave Newfield to find my queer community, but it was here all along. Wish I'd known."

Deb winces.

"It was a different time back then," she says. "Kind of don't ask, don't tell. I kept to myself, kept my private life private. But Jake and Gina were always breathing down my neck, terrified I'd have some horrible influence on you. I was banned from their place, which is why they loved hosting their Sunday dinners and having you sleep over there. They didn't want you down at the farm with me and the rest of my merry band of misfits. I sure got an earful after that kiss of yours. 'This is what you've always wanted, isn't it Deb? You finally turned that boy queer.'"

"But that's ridiculous! I had no idea about you! I thought I was the only one in the family."

"I know kid, and I'm sorry. If I could go back and do it different, I would. Maybe then it wouldn't have taken Dad's death to bring you home."

"What did Opa think about you and the others?" I ask quietly. "Was he okay with it?"

"He took some flack around town, but he always stood his ground. Love came first, with me and everybody else. Long as they were good, honest workers, they had a place at Wonder World. I don't know how many times I was able to set up someone in need with a gig, people who couldn't seem to get hired anywhere else, not even in the city. Dad was real good about that."

A weight I didn't know I was holding slides off my chest like a lead apron.

"Well, should we head back inside?" I ask. "I bet all your friends are missing you."

Deb stubs out her cigarette and reaches over to squeeze my hand. "You got it kid."

Inside, everyone is clustered around together, talking and laughing. I notice a framed photograph on a nearby table for the first time. It's me at five years old. I'm very awkwardly riding a sheep. My face is buried deep in its wool, taking in the scent of fresh grass and damp hay. Opa has a halter and a lead on the sheep, and he's walking beside me with a grin so wide you can see his gold-capped molar.

Deb catches my pause at the table and pats me on the shoulder.

"Found it in his office under some old papers a while back," she whispers. "Great shot of you two."

I lean into her for a breath, unable to say a word.

Jo is speaking. They raise their can of pop in our direction and welcome us into the circle.

"In my experience, most Mennonites don't know, or don't care to remember, how much they relied on my Métis ancestors to survive. We were their guides and midwives. We were displaced so they could make their home here. When I saw that ad in the paper, I wasn't so sure I wanted to work for a Mennonite. But Willie surprised me. He was open. He listened to me and was willing to educate himself. We had a good relationship. I'm glad to have known him."

Pearl takes a sip of her beer and steps forward.

"Everyone kept telling my parents to add cheeseburgers or ginger beef to the menu, 'something Newfield could understand.' But Willie ate what we offered, and he loved it. Lumpia and chicken adobo every Friday until we closed. When I needed a job to pay for college, I called him up and he said yes right away. Always asked after my mom and dad when he was making his rounds on one of my shifts. I'm going to miss him."

More voices join in.

"He drove me to work and back for a month straight, until I saved up enough to fix my clunker."

"He didn't give me any shit for having a mullet and a nose ring. I could always be myself around him."

"He made me feel like part of the family."

There are hands holding hands and fierce hugs amongst the sniffles. Carefree acts of queer love everywhere I look.

"I never met him, but I'm so glad he brought us all together."

Deb switches to water for the toasts, but I latch onto all the free drinks and float away on a river of suds. We reminisce until closing time, then past it. Eventually I realize most people have cleared out, and the fuzzy glow I've been cultivating all night is snuffed out.

Where am I going to sleep tonight?

I watch as Deb walks over to the bar and claims her keys from Sandy. Then she comes over to my table and reaches down to grab my bag.

"Ready to go, kid?"

There's a spark at the back of my head. The glow rushes past my ears and envelopes me once more.

"You sure? I don't want to put you out."

My aunt swings an arm around me and pulls us off towards the exit, refusing to entertain the question.

"Come on. We've got a lot to talk about."

There's only one vehicle left out in the parking lot, the rusty old half-tonne I noticed on my way in.

"I thought that must be Opa's truck!"

"Yep. Two hundred thousand klicks and still kicking. Hop in."

She tosses my stuff into the back and slides into the driver's seat. After some patient coaxing, the engine grumbles to life. I don't worry about the drive home because my aunt has always been the perfect mix of confident and cautious. Sure enough, she steers straight and goes the speed limit the whole way back to the farm even though nobody in the entire world, not even the RCMP, does ninety on St. Mary's.

As I tumble into the farmhouse, Deb doesn't try to stop me when I make the terrible decision to finish off the rest of my boxed wine. She just leaves the hallway lights on so I can find my way up to the spare room and says good night. When I reach the bed, I find the quilt turned down and two Alka-Seltzer tablets next to a glass of water on the nightstand. Five-star service, Auntie.

The elderly mattress sproings in complaint with each little move I make, but it doesn't bother me in the least. The last thing I remember before I'm fast asleep is the taste of salty tears running down my cheeks to meet the stupid grin on my face. There it is, finally. The feeling of home.

10

The sun reaches through the thin lace curtains and plucks out my eyeballs to pan-fry them. Downstairs, Deb is making breakfast. Every clinking dish and thudding drawer are like tiny depth charges dropped into my sloshing head. Morning, my old frenemy, we've got to stop meeting like this.

I down the fizzy glass of Alka-Seltzer and water set out for me, then cover my throbbing head with a pillow. Eventually, my need to pee overwhelms my raging hangover. I send a respectful request to my liquefied bones asking them to resolidify and, reluctantly, they comply.

I stumble down the creaking staircase and turn the corner. Expecting to find the bathroom, I find myself face-to-face with a snarling tiger instead. Deb rushes in with a wooden spoon brandished over her head when she hears me screaming bloody murder.

"Jeez, Isaac, you just about gave me a heart attack!"

"Sorry! Sorry," I say, clutching my heaving chest. "Wrong door."

One of Opa's quirkier business decisions was to taxidermy some of his animals after they passed and display them in a large room built onto the farmhouse. These glassy-eyed pelts used to give me the creeps when I stayed over. Kept thinking they would wake up in the night and eat me.

Still, you have to admire him. Only a Mennonite could figure out a way to keep making money off the corpses of his star attractions.

The tiger brothers take pride of place in the centre of the room, posed as if they're about to strike. There are many birds, including a full-sized emu, and the dusty heads of bison, an elk, and his famous giraffe have all been mounted to polished shields of wood. In the far corner, I even spot a one-eared tabby cat curled on top of a bearskin rug.

"God," I say with a groan. "He started doing the barn cats too? That's a bit much, isn't it?"

When I was a kid, there were always a rabble of half-feral felines prowling around the farm. They survived on whatever they could catch, from field mice to fallen corn dogs. I learned early on not to treat them like pets. Still have the scar on my left hand as a reminder of how sharp their claws could be. Opa used to joke even his tigers were afraid of those cats.

"Hey!" Deb exclaims. "How many times do I have to tell you not to nap in here!"

She stomps her foot. One of the cat's golden eyes briefly blazes at us with great contempt before blinking out again. Deb advances to prod the stubborn sleeper with her toe.

"Come on Dupps. You're not fooling anyone. It's time to get up. Breakfast is in your bowl."

At the word "bowl," the old tom rises with a yawn, revealing several jagged yellow teeth. His massive, shaggy belly drags on the ground as he stretches and saunters off towards the kitchen, leaving little bits of fur stuck to the bearskin in his wake.

"That's Dupps? I can't believe how big he's grown!"

Opa christened him Dupps, Plautdietsch for ass, because the precocious little cat was always such a pain in his. Dupps was only a kitten when I was in high school, but even then he had quite the reputation. His frequent attacks on Wonder World's guests caused much grief and many refunded ticket sales. He used to crawl onto the porch roof and lie in wait, pouncing on unsuspecting heads to snatch away baseball caps or some crying kid's teddy bear before tearing off into a field to shred the prize with his tiny claws. Even I began to wonder why Opa didn't just take the little hellion around back and shoot him, but that wasn't my grandfather's way.

Luckily, the cat did have his uses. One time our local MP, who was also the minister of finance, had his staff reach out to Opa. Apparently, he felt our tiger enclosure was the perfect backdrop for an important government funding announcement. There was just one problem. Opa hated the guy. It had something to do with a sour business deal from back in the days when the flashy parliamentarian was still a used car salesman. "He always knew how to sell you on a lemon, kjint. Now he's doing it for Ottawa." Of course, Opa had always been good at turning lemons into lemonade, so he permitted the spectacle to proceed on his property once the staffers agreed to pay triple our usual rental rate.

Everything ran smoothly until the wind picked up and Dupps mistook the minister's flapping toupee for a rival feline. A photo of the snarling kitten dive-bombing the hapless man's hairpiece made the front page of *The Free Press* the next day and national news the following evening, completely overshadowing whatever talking points the MP was trying to shill in his big announcement. Opa had lavishly doted on the one-eared tabby ever since. It's hard to believe this flabby old tom contently crunching his breakfast under the kitchen cupboards is the same cat. I guess even the most notorious rabble-rousers go into retirement eventually.

Deb slides me a plate of fried eggs on rye toast. She's kept a coop of chickens on the property since I was born, so I know this is going to be good.

"Might need to heat that up in the microwave," she says. "Wasn't expecting to eat so late."

That's a dig at me for sleeping in. It's only 7:30, but I need to remember the day starts at dawn around here. Deb must be well into her chores already.

"You'll be wanting coffee?" she asks.

"Sure, thanks."

Deb dumps out the remains of the last pot before lining the rust-stained coffee maker with a fresh filter. She pours a carafe's worth of water in the reservoir and reaches into the freezer for a jumbo container of Maxwell House. The room is quickly filled with a dark and heady aroma, sharp as a knife and slightly burnt at the edges. It's the kind of coffee you can only get from a pot that never stops percolating, poured out at twenty-four-hour diners, small-town mechanics, and one former game farm located thirty-five klicks south of Winnipeg.

When the brew is ready, I drink deeply to clear the fog in my head. Sunlight pours into the kitchen as we finish our drinks, painting the room the rich orangey yellow of a farm-fresh double yolker. A satisfied moan gurgles up from deep in my belly.

"Thank you. I needed that."

"Suppose so, after a night like yours. Now that you're up, should we talk about your inheritance?"

I grip my mug more tightly and ask the question that's been on my mind since Abe first told me about the will.

"You and your brothers must be pretty pissed, huh?"

"Not at all!" she says, giving her work pants an emphatic slap. "You know Dad sold most of his land over the years, and he built up quite an impressive investment portfolio with the profits. You'd have to sell this property to see any money, but us kids get to split whatever's left in his accounts after expenses are taken care of. Trust me, we'll all be fine. More than. Nobody's hurting here."

"Did Opa leave a note or anything? About why he wanted me specifically to have the farm?"

Deb shakes her head. "We never even knew he changed his will. Still thought Jake was executor, until Dad passed and I got the call instead. Somehow, he managed to get in touch with his lawyer after he went into the home. That was quite a feat, let me tell you, seeing how short a leash my brother and his wife kept him on. I was lucky to get in a visit once every couple of months. Tried to tell me he was too frail for visitors, but that was bullshit. They just didn't want me to see him."

"That's awful! Must have driven you crazy being just down the road from him."

"Sure did, but what could I do? Gina's head aide and Jake's the mayor. They've got this whole town under their thumb."

I swirl a finger through a ring of coffee on the table, trying to choose my next words carefully. "I never pictured Opa ending up in Sunset Villa. Thought he'd be running Wonder World until the day he died. Was there an accident?"

Abruptly, Deb stands up and throws our breakfast dishes onto the counter. She fills the sink with soap and scalding water, then drowns the plates and gives them an aggressive scrub down. Eventually she tells me, without turning around, about finding Opa on his back in the yard, snowflakes gently kissing his blue chattering lips. He'd gone out to feed the animals like he did every morning, and when he didn't return right away, she figured he'd gone into his shop to tinker around. But he'd slipped on a patch of black ice just outside the chicken coop, shattering the eggs in his hands as well as his left hip.

Jake and Gina descended before the paramedics were even dispatched from St. Stache. They'd been saying for years it was time for Opa to sell the farm and move into town, but he'd resisted and so had Deb. She swore she could take care of him just fine where he was. Not that he needed much help. Willie was in better shape than many Newfield men half his age. The ones who grew soft and doughy as the vereniki they piled on their plates during business luncheons at Oma's Kitchen.

A busted hip was a different story, though. Jake and Gina moved Opa into a private suite at Sunset Villa as soon as the hospital discharged him. It was a moonless night, and his last glimpse of Wonder World was the flickering yard light casting shadows on his snow-covered truck. He was in that retirement home for five years but never set foot on his farm again.

The dull ache of regret throbs in my chest. No one thought to phone me after his accident, but even if they had, I probably wouldn't have answered. All this lost time, and nothing to do but live with it.

"Jake's had a plan for this land a long time now," Deb says. "Wants to leave a lasting mark on the town. Some kind of big development that would attract new business, double the population. He sure was hopping mad when he heard about Dad's new will. Until he read the catch, of course."

"What catch?"

"You don't know? Dad said you've got to live here, in the house, for at least six months straight to inherit the farm. If you don't, we revert back to the old will, and my brothers and I split it three ways just like with the cash. We didn't have a clue how to contact you. If Abe hadn't tracked you down ..."

"The mayor would've gotten his wish."

"Exactly."

Guess that explains Jake and Gina's attempted niceties at the funeral, as well as their cheerful send off when I decided to leave. If I know my uncle, he'll be cooking up some new scheme to get his way now that I'm back in the picture. When it comes to money and power, that guy's like a pig to garbage. You don't get down in the mud with Jake Funk if you can help it.

"But what do I do now?" I ask. "It cost me everything I had just to fly out here. If I can't sell the farm right away, I'm hooped."

Deb flinches slightly at this remark. "You've got some time before you can make any decisions like that, yes, but there's plenty to do around here in the interim. Most of the animals are gone, but there's still the chickens. And I've been doing a weekly market stall to help make ends meet the last couple of years. Can't pay much, but you help me out and I'll give you a cut. How's that sound?"

There's a sudden brush of fur against my leg. I look down and see Dupps circling around my chair to rub his other cheek against my calf. He must feel I'm worth claiming as part of his territory. The old tom pads over to a well-worn rug under the sink and flops down with a contented sigh for a nap. His purrs reverberate outwards towards us.

"I would love that. Thanks for the advice, Deb, and for being so kind about all of this. I really appreciate it."

She clears her throat. "Well alright then. If you'll excuse me, I'm running a bit behind on my morning chores."

"You want any help?"

"When you're ready, kid," she says, already on her way out. "Don't want to rush you. I'll be in the shop."

I'd say that's Deb Speak for *Yes, your royal highness, time to get off your ass and lend a hand.*

The next three weeks breeze by. Adjusting to farm life is easier than I thought. Sure, I'm exhausted at the end of every day, but it's nice to work with my hands again. There's no landlord to dodge or late-night sirens to wake me up or buses to run after in the rain. All I have to do is complete the task in front of me and then the next one and the next until it's time to collapse on the couch with a cold beer. Doesn't leave me much time to think. Right now, that's a good thing.

Gossip travels faster than fibre optic internet in Mennoland, so I'm sure my family knows I'm here, but I haven't heard a peep from Abe, Gina, or the mayor since I moved in with Deb. If they expect me to reach out first, they're in for a long wait. In the meantime, there's always something to keep myself busy: lawns to mow, gardens to weed, berry bushes to water. Deb's Saturday stall at the St. Norbert Farmers' Market attracts hordes of Winnipeg hipsters who eagerly thrust their wads of cash at us in exchange for fresh fruits and veggies, folksy preserves, and flats of eggs.

Course, I doubt they'd be so ovum obsessed if they ever went picking with me. I'd forgotten how much it reeks inside a chicken coop. The first time I went in to collect the day's bounty, I nearly hawked my Cheezies all over the shit-covered floor. It wasn't just the smell that bothered me. Free-range chickens might be trendy, but I'd rather have those squawking birds locked in cages than running around at my feet. Those assholes can *peck* if you get too close.

11

As soon as Deb hands over my first paycheque, I'm itching to spend it at the MCC thrift shop. Thrifting is one of my favourite pastimes, and there's no better place than Mennoland for a second-hand shopper. The MCC offers everything from half-burned candles to chesterfields with pre-grooved ass padding. Plus, each item you buy saves an orphan. Or buys them a goat. Or something. There's nothing the discerning Newfield consumer likes more than mixing good deals with good deeds.

The volunteer Omas who stock MCC's shelves don't have a clue about brand names, so genuine Levi's have always been priced the same as Tante Loeppky's homemade jean skirt. I had some serious sticker shock the first time I went thrifting on the East Coast. First it took over an hour to bus from my dorm room at Dal to the Value Village in Bayer's Lake, and then the bastards wanted thirty bucks for a mismatched set of threadbare sheets! Halifax had plenty of vintage, consignment, and antique shops, but none of them offered bag sale days where you could get a whole new wardrobe for seven bucks. Now that I'm back in town, nothing's going to keep me from this sweet cheap merchandise.

On the day of the sale, I wake early and corner my aunt in the kitchen.

"Hey Deb, where are the keys to the truck?"

"In my pocket."

I hold out my hand. "Well, can I have them?"

She takes a long slow slurp of her coffee before responding. "Nope. Got some errands to run today."

"Oh shoot. I was hoping to hit up the MCC. I could zip into town real quick, be back before you need to head out?"

She shakes her head. "Jo's already on their way. We're busy all afternoon. Sorry."

"Well, what am I going to do then?"

"You're a smart kid," she says, heading out the door with the truck keys jangling ever so tantalizingly from her back pocket. "Figure it out."

And this is how I find myself huffing and puffing towards Newfield on a rusted-out bicycle I found behind the barn.

Growing up in a place where everything shuts down by nine p.m., you have to make your own fun. I don't know how many times Neth and I crisscrossed Newfield by bike or foot as kids just to fill those elastic hours between supper and bedtime. As soon as I got old enough to borrow Abe's car we bolted for the big city, making late-night runs to McDick's or catching a flick at the cheap seats on McGillivray.

Then there was the really stupid shit we'd get up to, like car tag. Neth and I invented the game one night when we were too short on cash for a trip to Winnipeg, and it quickly caught on with the rest of our grade. To play, everyone would divide into groups and pile into a couple of cars. One team was it and the other would go hide somewhere around town. The object of the game was to corner the other car so one of your passengers could get out and tap their hood before the opposing driver could peel away. It was stupid and totally dangerous, but at least it kept our boredom at bay.

From Sunday to Friday, I had to shoehorn myself into the kind of person I was supposed to be, practising the piano and getting good grades. But Saturday nights? That's when I let loose.

I was willing to try anything that could help me shake off my humdrum life and feel truly alive. The thrill of independence was short-lived of course. At the stroke of midnight our curfews would kick in and our carriages would turn back into beetroots. I hated those drives back to town. Felt like reporting to prison for a crime I didn't commit.

At last, the saggy bald tires of my bike thump-bump over the railroad tracks marking Newfield's western edge. I used to watch the trains going by on their way from Winnipeg to North Dakota with grain cars hauling wheat and graffiti. I wanted to spray paint my own message on them. *SOS. Stuck in Mennoland. Will trade borscht for beer.* But nothing stopped here. The outside world rumbled right on past, forever out of reach.

After giving my all to get into town, I decide to grab a snack at Oma's Kitchen before heading over to the thrift shop. There's a waitress having a smoke out back when I pull into the parking lot. Her neon red hair clashes delightfully with the café uniform, a stiff white apron and orange dress hemmed a chaste length below the knee.

"Nice ride PK," she says with a snicker as I lean my shitty bike against the building.

I flip through my mental yearbook to try and place her. PK, short for Pastor's Kid, was my nickname back in high school. I hated it and tried to make Treblemaker stick instead. I thought it was a nice nod to the piano and my reputation as a weekend partier, but everybody else said it was super dumb. Neth did give it a try for a week before switching back to Funk. I loved her for that.

Desperate to avoid small talk and still coming up short on the server's name, I offer only an awkward smile and wave before heading inside the café for some major déjà vu. The greasy spoon still has the same peeling wallpaper and cracked vinyl booths packed close for easy eavesdropping. As always, there is the steady hum of conversation from a crowd of locals downing cup after cup of self-serve coffee as they rubberneck Main Street and pass along the day's gossip.

The top seller at Oma's Kitchen is their chicken bucket, which is deep-fried in oil that definitely isn't changed every five thousand kilometres. Just a second inside the place is enough to saturate you in the café's signature perfume: a blend of grease, sweat, and smoke from back when you could still light up in restaurants. As the only place to eat left in town, they also offer pizza, pasta, and all-day breakfasts.

One plus of growing up without a mom was that Abe never subjected Loreena to the café's Mother's Day Feast, also known as The Saddest Buffet In The History Of The World. I remember walking by these big picture windows as a kid one dreary spring day after church and seeing all those poor women stoically enduring an inadequate gesture of appreciation from husbands who were too lazy, cheap, or forgetful to make a reservation someplace nice in the city. Behind them, their unwatched children fought each other for the last piece of cheese pizza slowly dying under the buffet's flickering heat lamps.

I spot Pearl on her lunch break with some coworkers. She's an aide at Sunset Villa now. Deb told me Pearl helped her keep tabs on Opa while he was in there, a small kindness my aunt was very grateful for. We exchange a friendly nod before I snag a stool at the singles counter.

"So, what'll it be?" the server asks when she returns from her smoke break.

"Chicken fingers with honey-dill sauce. And just water to drink, thanks."

"Classic PK budget combo," she says with a wink. "You haven't changed a bit."

There's a plastic name tag affixed to her apron reading "Steph P." Ah hah! The Plett girl.

The last time I saw Steph P. she had a bright purple fauxhawk and we were in the middle of making out. It was the last Friday night kegger before graduation at our usual hangout in the woods outside town. We were playing some weird drinking game, a hybrid of Strip Twister and Seven Minutes in Heaven, and the hormones and hard-ons were raging. She tasted like raspberries and I asked if she'd been eating jam but she laughed and held up an empty bottle of flavoured vodka. There were four Stephanies in my grade, so we always included the last initial when they were mentioned. Judging by the name tag, I guess at least half of them must have ended up working here after high school. Party.

"Thought you left town," she says when she brings my food.

"I did, yeah. Now I'm back."

"Cool. Welcome home."

I want to tell her I don't really like to call this place home, but she's already moved onto another table.

"No worries," she tells a woman whose daughter has just spilled a drink. "I'll clean that right up for you, darling. Got two at home myself. Gotta love them, right?"

Shit, two? I start doing the math on how many kids our grade has likely produced by this point and then stop because it's depressing as hell.

I give Steph P. a decent tip when I go. She writes her number down on my bill and offers another wink on my way out the door. Guess some people never change.

At the thrift shop, my eye is drawn to a pair of gloriously hideous jeans. I hold them up to my hips and instantly fall in love with their high-waisted, pocketless, acid wash perfection. The denim's the kind of soft you can only get after a thousand trips through the washer, and they seem to be a perfect fit.

There's only one problem. My presence under the hand-painted *Ladies Clothing* sign has disturbed a family of frowning Hutterites. The mother and her five daughters look like a set of nesting dolls with their matching brown hair, long dresses, and polka-dotted head coverings. I let go of the mom jeans and move off towards my assigned section. The women return to their shopping once they're sure I've found my proper place.

With so much new stock being donated every day, MCC is concerned with maximizing their storage space, not their profits. Even on the men's side there's plenty to pick through, though I bypass the second-hand underwear bin with its jumble of thinning cotton and over-stretched elastic. I may be on a budget, but I still have standards.

I grab work clothes for the farm and a couple of cute tops before sneaking back for the jeans when I'm sure nobody's watching. At the checkout, an elderly volunteer pulls out a crinkly shopping bag from beneath the counter and stuffs my purchases in until it's fit to burst. She does this without speaking or looking up. I know this tactic well. It's the kind of skillful detachment one adopts after performing a thankless and repetitive task for an extended period of time. I wonder if she spent her working life at one of the local slaughterhouses. The powerful motions of her wrists while wrangling my clothes could just as easily pinion a panicked chicken.

Satisfied with my thrifting haul, I zip off down Main Street in the direction of the farm. Before I can make my getaway though, someone pokes their head out of the town office and calls out.

"Isaac!"

The shopping bag catches in the spokes of my bike and I nearly do a face plant.

"Sorry to startle you!" my uncle booms. "But do you have a moment?"

It's colder than a morgue inside the town office. Despite their cardigans and floor-length skirts, Jake's employees shiver at their desks. There's a lock on the thermostat, and I'm sure I know who holds the key. The mayor walks me past a long line of filing cabinets and a community bulletin board overflowing with ads for tractor parts, church fundraisers, and free zucchini.

"Make yourself comfortable," he says, ushering me into the

council chambers. "I'll be back in a moment. If you'd like coffee or water just let one of the girls know."

Yes, because I'm sure that's part of their job description. "I'm good, thanks."

I plunk my thrifted clothes down on a plush leather chair with a bronze name plate marked *Councillor Goertzen* and take in the room. A Manitoba flag stands at attention in the corner. Frosted windows hide Main Street from view. The far wall features a gallery of municipal government mug shots, row after row of white men in black suits. The sausage party is broken up only once, by a stern-looking woman with large glasses, even larger hair, and a shoulder-padded pantsuit. The inscription below lists her as *Mrs. Albert Stoesz*, so I'm guessing she didn't exactly run on a platform of radical feminist reform.

Mayor Jake returns with an armful of blueprints and graphs and launches into a presentation more polished than the chamber's gleaming oak table. His smile never falters as he pivots to address each part of the empty room like we're in a screen test for *Dragon's Den*. It's hard to keep my mind from wandering the longer he drones on.

Greener Pastures Property Group. Motivated investors. Unprecedented growth.

"Yes."

Competitive pricing. Triple the tax base. Franchise opportunities.

"Sure."

Contractors. Permits. Rezoning.

"Can I ask a question?"

"Of course, of course," my uncle says with a chuckle. "Listen to me rambling on. I'm just so darn excited!"

I pick up one of his glossy brochures and study it more closely. A multicoloured blob oozes over a map of Opa's farmland. Red for residential. Green for recreation. Yellow for commercial. Blue for light industry. The edges of the blob protrude towards Newfield, threatening to swallow the town whole.

"Why Riverview Terrace?" I ask. "Wonder World is miles from the Red."

"That's just good marketing. We're trying to sell folks on that slow-paced country lifestyle while at the same time offering every amenity of the big city."

"Sounds like false advertising to me."

Mayor Jake waves the comment away. "We can always incorporate a water feature into the plans if need be. You know, I was reading in the paper just the other day how much trouble the government is having with that abandoned ship up near Selkirk. Needs to be scrapped, but nobody wants to pay for it. We could build a new lake to rival St. Stache. Haul the wreck down here and offer scuba diving lessons so people can explore it. I'm telling you, the opportunities are endless!"

"What about the farmhouse?"

"You mean our new strip mall!" the mayor corrects me. "I have connections with a local storage facility. We can save anything you want before the demolition, but we're going to need every inch of the place to bring our vision to life.

"I'd imagine a young, uh, urban fellow such as yourself would want to relocate to Toronto or Vancouver after the sale, but I'd be happy to talk with my business partners about a healthy lot discount if you'd like to get in with us here on the ground floor. Phase one has some nice quiet cul-de-sacs. I could see you settling in nicely with one of our deluxe duplexes on Cattail Close or Lilypad Lane. Huge resale potential, and of course the commute to Winnipeg would still be quite manageable. You see? There's a solution to every problem. Now, anything else I can help clear up for you?"

He locks eyes with me, and I hold his gaze for a moment before speaking.

"Yeah, there is actually. Did you ever pitch Opa Willie on this idea?"

A shadow passes over my uncle's face.

"I suppose it may have come up once or twice. Why do you ask?"

"Well, Opa had a good head for business. If this deal is as great as you say it is, he wouldn't have turned it down. Not unless he disagreed with the overall concept. Is that why he left the land to me and not to you? Help me out, Uncle Jake. What am I missing here?"

The mayor's gums tighten their grip around his artificially whitened teeth.

"You know, Nephew, if there's one thing I'll regret the rest of my life, it's the fact that I left my father's care in the hands of others for far too long. That man gave everything to his family, and I should have done more to say thanks. But he didn't like asking for help, and I didn't want to push.

"I should've paid closer attention to what was going on out on that farm. Your poor frail grandfather was far too easy to influence in his final years. A man like that with a portfolio like his, you never know what kind of vultures might be lurking about, ready to prey on a fragile mind.

"But it's like the good book says. What men intend for evil, God can use for good. When I saw the lengths my brother went to track you down after all this time, it touched my heart. Sure, we could spend a small fortune asking a judge to decide which will is legally legitimate, but what sense would that make? I believe my father wanted this family to come together and share the wealth. And with your help, Isaac, that's exactly what I intend to do."

My hands are melding to my chair in this artificial cold. I shake them out and stand, desperate to reclaim some warmth. Mayor Jake rises alongside me.

"I think it's time I get back to the farm," I say. "Don't want to fall too far behind on my chore list."

"Well, you've certainly inherited that strong Funk work ethic, haven't you? But tell me, before you go, have you spoken with your aunt about what the land is worth yet?"

"No, but I should really—"

"Half a million, easy. And that's just the starting bid. My partners wouldn't want me sharing this, but family comes first. I could make a few discreet calls and find you an excellent negotiating team. Sky's the limit for a shrewd young businessman like yourself."

"I ... didn't realize."

Zeroes upon zeroes dance in front of my eyes, momentarily blurring my vision. The mayor senses my hesitation and ups his folksy salesman charm.

"My dear nephew, I think it's admirable you want to honour your grandfather's wishes. But I've read this new will from front to back and there's nothing, not even a footnote, about what's to be done with the land once your six-month stay is up. Taking care of a property that size is no easy task. Lord knows my sister's struggled to keep up with it all, but she's too stubborn to ask for my help. You and I though? That's a clean slate. It's time for cooler heads to prevail. There's no reason we can't both be winners here. It's what my father would want, trust me."

Five hundred thousand dollars? Goodbye student loans, credit card debt, shitty rentals with asshole landlords. This is my chance to start over.

"I need time to think," I say, snatching my MCC bag and heading for the exit. "I'll talk it over with Deb and get back to you."

My uncle lets me pass but clears his throat with purpose just as my fingers grasp the frosty chamber doorknob.

"I'd be very careful about the council I keep if I were you, Isaac. All I want is for both of us to walk away from this deal rich men. Have you stopped to consider what your aunt's motivations might be?"

"Deb just wants me to be happy."

Mayor Jake snorts. "Is that what she's told you? Well, I'm glad to hear it. I just hope it's true. Because it's been my experience, Nephew, that when it comes to money, everyone's got their angle. If they say they don't, they're probably lying. As you can see, I'm quite happy to lay my cards on the table. Perhaps it's time for my sister to do the same.

"My plans for this property might seem a bit ambitious, but the upsides are clear. We both know this town's caused you pain, but it's a pain I can ease. Just take my advice. Stay the six months, cash my cheque, and go live your life however you choose. Someplace where you belong."

Walking out into the heat of the open air, a numbness lingers in my limbs like I've been shot through with novocaine. My uncle sure knows how to yank my emotions out by the roots. His bluntness was uncomfortable, but what if he's right? If time can't heal all wounds, maybe cold hard cash is worth a try.

12

Back at the farm, I'm greeted by a flurry of shingles falling from the sky. Two figures kneel on the roof of the old barn, tossing hunks of material into a dumpster positioned below them.

I raise my voice to be heard above all the banging and thudding and the tinny strains of some classic rock song.

"What are you doing?"

A face peaks over the edge of the roof. It's Jo. "Hey, Isaac!"

My aunt pops up beside her friend. "We're redoing the roof," Deb explains.

"Why?"

"It's a nice day for it and Jo was free."

"No, I mean why now? Is this really necessary?"

"Well, yes, actually. Barn's been in need of some TLC awhile now. There a problem?"

"You should have consulted me," I say, squinting up at her. "Like, how much is all this going to cost? We don't use the barn for anything right now, so why bother fixing it up? If you'd asked me, I'd have said to leave it for the new owners to worry about."

Deb rests back on her haunches and reaches over to turn off her portable radio.

"Hey, Jo," she says. "You mind doing a Timmy's run? I sure could use a coffee right about now."

Jo nods and slips their work gloves into their back pocket.
"No problem."

"Appreciate it. Keys are in the truck," Deb says before turning
back to me. "Hold the ladder, kid. We're coming down."

"You still like honey crullers?" Jo asks me as they clomp down
the metal rungs.

"Sure, thanks."

I offer them a fiver, but they smile it away.

"This one's on me. What are friends for, hey?"

Deb waits until the truck is kicking up dust on its way to
St. Stache before speaking. "Now that we're alone, mind telling
me what's got your panties in a bunch?"

"Is it so unreasonable to expect a head's up when my farm is
in need of major repairs?" I sputter.

Deb lights a cigarette and takes a deep breath. Her response is
quiet and measured, though she can't keep a vein from popping
in her forehead.

"I didn't realize you were planning to take over all the property
management duties so soon," she says. "Certainly would have saved
me a lot of elbow grease to let you handle the roof. For the record,
the shingles were ordered back in the spring when Dad was still
alive and I was looking after the place on his behalf, not yours.
But this is Jo's busy season, and they didn't have time to help until
today. You're welcome to try returning everything if you like, along
with the paint for the house and the new chicken wire for the coop.
I'm sure the receipts are buried somewhere in Dad's office. But I
see more than dollar signs when I look at this place, so if that's
your approach, then maybe it's best I find someplace else to stay."

"No! Don't do that. Please."

Deb's right, I'm being an ass. She and Opa poured decades of
their lives into this place. It must break her heart to see her dad's
dream slowly falling apart. There's no way she could keep up with
all the repairs by herself, but that hasn't stopped her from trying.

"Do you mind if we sit?" I ask, jerking my head towards the porch swing. "I could use some shade."

Deb regards me for a moment, then stomps out her butt and follows me towards the house.

I let the old swing squeak back and forth a bit before continuing our conversation. "I owe you an apology. You're looking out for me and I'm grateful for all the help. I wouldn't have a clue how to take care of this place without you."

"You're smart. You'd figure it out eventually."

"No. I really wouldn't."

I grab the rusty coffee tin that serves as the porch's ashtray and plop it down between us, holding my hand out for a cigarette. We both light up.

"Where's all this new owner talk coming from anyway?" she asks. "You haven't said boo about the will since your first night here."

"I know. I've been trying to take it all in. But Jake cornered me when I was in town and made his big sales pitch for Riverview Terrace."

The vein in Deb's forehead pops again. She mutters something I can't make out.

"What's that?" I ask.

She ignores my question. "What'd he offer for the land?"

A twinge of suspicion goes through my gut, but I ignore it. Deb's been nothing but helpful and kind this whole month.

"Half a million."

She laughs, but with a harder edge than I'm expecting. "That lowballing son of a gun."

"What?"

"Kid, I'm going to book you an appointment with a local appraiser this week so you can hear it straight from the horse's mouth, but this place could easily go for twenty or twenty-five grand an acre. Don't let my brother razzle dazzle you. Half a million dollars sure sounds great, but you could get four times that on the market right now. It's your prerogative to sell the farm if that's what you want, but take the time your opa's given you and do your homework. Don't do something you'll regret just to make a quick buck."

"Did you ever make plans for this place beyond Wonder World?" I ask.

Deb takes a long drag on her cigarette before responding.

"We used to go camping together," she says. "All the Triple L folks. But we got tired of getting the stink eye at the beach and those random noise complaints when all we were doing was sitting around a fire having a quiet beer. So we stopped.

"Sure, I dreamed about having a place where we could all go and be ourselves. Even came up with a business plan to turn the farm into a retreat centre. I thought maybe we could put a kitchen and a dining hall into the barn, host dances or socials on the weekends. Build some nice cabins for people to stay in.

"I wanted to tell Dad. Could've given him odd jobs to keep him busy. Wouldn't have been as taxing as the game farm was. But something always held me back. And then he had his accident. So that was that."

Deb taps her ash into the tin.

"Anyway, all that's in the past now. I'll tell you what. How 'bout I keep you in the loop on any outstanding projects around here, and you agree not to chew me out about them in front of my friends. Deal?"

"Deal."

We shake hands. A smile tugs at the corners of my aunt's mouth.

"Good talk," she says. "Now, if you'll excuse me, I've got a roof to reshingle."

"Want any help?"

She shakes her head. "Jo and I can handle it. Why don't you take the night off, see what that high school buddy of yours is up to?"

"You mean Neth?" I ask. "Actually, that's not a bad idea."

A long, castigating yowl emanates from inside the house. Dupps appears at the screen door and fixes us with a death glare.

Deb and I exchange a look of amusement.

"And maybe feed the cat?" I ask.

"And maybe feed the cat," she replies.

I text Neth about catching a movie and, wonder of wonders, she's actually free for once.

> OMG YESSSSSSSS!!! I'll pick you up!!! she messages.

> lol! what movie you wanna see tho? I reply.

> who cares?? its a night out! just no princesses, pirates or paw patrol...gimme that sweet sweet SEX n VIOLEnCE!

> you got it chicky. ;)

We've been trying to hang out since I got back to town, but Neth's free time is at a premium between work and her kids. Connor's no help. He runs a small painting company and avoids the house as much as possible. Apparently, he's always texting Neth last minute about some unexpected overtime or drinks with his buddies, leaving her to sort things out at home. If he texts at all.

Sitters are expensive, and though Neth's mom has offered to babysit, that too comes at a price. Mrs. Kehler always brings a creepy illustrated bible from the fifties with her, which scares the bejesus out of the kids. I guess tonight Neth must figure some time with me is worth any nightmares she'll have to deal with when she gets back.

Her kids have a meltdown when they hear she's leaving. They like surprises about as much as they like storytime with Oma. I tell her it's no problem; we can catch the late show instead. She peels into the farmyard at quarter to nine, blasting Metric from her minivan's blown out speakers just like old times. When we get to St. Vital, we order root beer and popcorn with extra butter and laugh like maniacs as the hero of our action flick slashes, shoots, and smooches his way through two hours and fourteen minutes of Hollywood horseshit. An older couple glares at us on our way out of the theatre and Neth sticks her tongue out at them, which launches us into another giggle fit. We're back in her van for a grand total of five seconds when she smacks the wheel and announces she's craving a McFlurry.

"With extra pickles on top for baby?" I joke as we enter the drive-thru line.

She gives me a playful shove. "Dork."

We idle in the parking lot for a few more minutes while we devour our treats.

"God!" Neth moans as she finishes the last bite of her dessert. "I'd forgotten how frigging good this crap is. Haven't been to McDick's in years!"

"Really?"

"Dude, I never leave town anymore. Doesn't matter how many toys and games I pack; my kids always fight like crazy whenever they're in the car. I still can't believe I drove all the way to the city without anyone screaming or kicking my seat."

"I can definitely hop in the back and raise some hell if you want," I offer.

She laughs. "It's good to have you back, Funk. How's things out at the farm?"

Neth already knows about the will and my job with Deb, but I update her on my uncle's offer to take the place off my hands when my six-month stay is up.

"Shit," she says when I finish. "That's a lot of money. You going to say yes?"

"Honestly? I don't know yet. It's so weird imagining myself being on the same side as the mayor about anything."

"I can see that. He still hasn't apologized for kicking you out of church, has he?"

I shake my head. "But it's not just that. I don't want to kick

Deb out after all she's done for the place, and I want to do right by my opa too. It just seems wrong to tear Wonder World down for some shoddy condos and another gas station. But what the hell do I know? I've been gone for ten years. Maybe this is what people want."

"Everybody loved Wonder World," Neth says. "But it's totally your decision. I'm behind you whatever happens, and I'm sure your family will be too."

Neth's phone buzzes in her purse. She makes a face as she looks at the screen.

"Trouble?" I ask.

"It's Connor. He doesn't like hanging out in the house with my mom if I'm not there, but he's had a few too many to look after the kids on his own."

"Shoot, I'm sorry. Should we go?"

She crumples up our bag of fast food and tosses it in the back. "Guess so."

It's well after midnight by the time Neth drops me off at the farm. I send her a text about half an hour later.

everything cool over there?

just peachy she replies. apparently Oma Kehler introduced my kids to jael's tent peg tonight...we were supposed to go camping for august long and now they're terrified. thanks mom!!! Also came home to this:

A Himalaya of dirty dishes fill my screen.

I picture her house, every hungry mouth asleep except one. There's a light on in the kitchen, silhouetting a solitary woman in yellow rubber gloves. Her tired hands plunge into the sink again and again, scrubbing cutlery and plates that will soon be crusted over with tomorrow's egg yolks and ketchup. All I can offer is a heart emoji.

Urgent scratching and several insistent mews greet me around noon the next day.

"Just a minute Dupps!" I cry out and roll over.

But the old tom is not to be ignored. The scratching intensifies and is soon joined by a strange new sound.

"What the hell is that?"

I spring out of bed to find the cat pulling at a note under my door. I slam a hand down and yank it back before he can shred any more of the paper.

> *Morning, kid.*
>> *Give me a call when you can. Just heading to St. Stache*
>> *Emerg. Looked after the chickens for you but cat'll probably*
>> *want food.*
> —*Deb*

"Oh good, you're up," she says when I reach her. "Have a nice night with your friend?"

"What's going on? You alright?"

"Course. *I* know how to use a ladder."

"What does that mean?"

"I'm here with your father. He had a little accident. Broke his leg, actually." She pauses to let me get out an expletive before continuing. "Yes, well. The doctors would like to keep him here for a while, and I was wondering if you could bring him an overnight bag so I can come back to the farm. There's rain in the forecast on Friday, and I'd like to get some more work done on the barn if I can."

I fling open the door and nearly fly headlong down the stairs thanks to Dupps.

"I'll feed you in a minute!" I say, twisting around the petulant cat. "Wait, Deb, if you have the truck, what am I going to do? Bike all the way to St. Stache?"

"Course not. You can take your dad's car. I left a set of keys in his mailbox."

"Why didn't you wake me?"

"Everything was under control," she replies. "And you had a late night. No need to worry, just bring that bag. I'll text you the list."

She hangs up before I can grill her for more details. The thermometer in the kitchen says it's already thirty-one out, and the temperature is still rising. It's going to be a brutal ride into town. Dupps follows me into the room and sinks his teeth into my heel when I try to sidestep him. I curse and spritz my foot with rubbing alcohol while dumping an ample serving of food into the cat's bowl.

Maybe I'll ask for a check up after they fit the old man with his cast. What a fan-fucking-tastic day for the Funk family.

13

As a combined dental clinic, eye doctor, family practice, blood lab, emergency department, and ten-bed hospital, the Saint-Eustache-sur-la-Rivière Regional Health Centre has a little something for everyone. The squat brick building hunches over a cramped parking lot, its insides a maze of windowless hallways the colour of pea soup. It's not a popular place to work. I must have seen a dozen different GPs here as a kid.

In the dilapidated reception area, a clerk using a pot of wilted flowers to catch a ceiling leak says my old man is in room three without looking up from their Sudoku game. Evidently Abe's room is close to the kitchen, as the stink of boiled turnip is strong down his hallway. He's lucky enough to have a window with a charming view of an overflowing dumpster. Someone's taped an *Out of Order* sign on the tiny television mounted to a swivel arm above his bed. There are no chairs and the bench in the hall is bolted to the floor. I'm overwhelmed with patriotic gratitude for the opulent largesse of our nation's public healthcare system.

I pick a spot on the wall to lean against and keep watch over Abe, who is fast asleep under an orange, green, purple, and brown afghan. I recognize this as one of Oma Trudy's creations. Deb must have brought it from home. I've been told my grandmother wasn't one to waste a scrap of yarn. Her blankets may not be much to look at, but they've kept our family warm for more than fifty years.

Abe's left leg is encased in a cast from ankle to mid-thigh, and there's a large bandage on his forehead. Without meaning to, I find the rhythm of my breathing has slowed to match his. Eventually, the old man stirs.

"I was having the strangest dream," he murmurs.

"Hello to you too," I reply. "How're you feeling?"

"I jumped out a plane."

"Very funny. Is that how this happened?"

I gently knock on his broken leg. His gown is thin and short, exposing the pasty flesh above his thigh. I realize this is the first time I've seen this particular part of his body. The old man hasn't donned swimming trunks or shorts as long as I've known him.

"No, no." He chuckles. "I was rummaging around in the crawl-space above the garage and lost my footing on the extension ladder. These things happen. Did I ever tell you about the time Loreena went skydiving?"

I can't remember the last time Abe said my mother's name out loud. How hard did he hit his head?

"I don't think so, no."

"It was just before your first birthday. I was sure she'd break her neck and we'd have a funeral instead of a party, but she was bound and determined."

"You mean you weren't tempted to go along?" I ask, wanting to make the most of this rare disclosure. "I'm shocked!"

Abe snorts at this. "Couldn't make you an orphan, could I?"

"Was this in Winnipeg?"

"Nä, Steinbach," he continues. "Close by the Mennonite Heritage Village there. Your mother asked for the highest altitude, of course. Eleven thousand feet. Can you imagine? I was watching from a field. Praying. You were there too. Slept in your car seat the whole time."

"Too young to know fear," I joke.

"They took a photo of her landing. Must have been part of the package. Parachute streaming out behind her, hair sticking out every which way, all lit up by the sun. I'd never seen her smile so big, not even on our wedding day."

"Is that what you were looking for above the garage? Her picture?"

Abe's face suddenly snaps shut like a book. He reaches for some water but gets caught up in his IV line.

"Here, let me." I pick up the cup and tilt it towards his open lips. "How long did you have to wait before Deb found you?"

"Took awhile to reach the phone, but she got there quick as she could."

"Why didn't you call an ambulance?"

"Your aunt got me here just fine," he shifts slightly, wincing as he bumps his cast against the bedframe. "Did you bring my things?"

I hand over the bag. He rifles down to the bottom but comes up empty handed with a sigh.

"Did I forget something?" I ask.

"Just my bible," he says, like another person would say "Just my oxygen tank" or "Just my prosthetic leg."

"Sorry. I can bring it tomorrow if you like."

He sinks back into his pillow. "If you can."

A sharp rap at the door interrupts us. My gaydar blips as a handsome doctor strides into the room. The man is tall and toned, probably in his mid-thirties, with manscaped brows and slicked back pompadour hair. Sadly, the metrosexual vibes turn out to be a false positive. As soon as he opens his mouth, I can tell we don't bat for the same team. Doctor Douchebag speaks with a casual kind of swaggering authority only a straight white man could pull off.

"Mr. Funk! Back so soon, are we?"

"So soon?" I echo.

"Yes, we had an appointment just last week. I'm also his GP," the man explains. "We medical professionals have to wear a lot of hats in these small-town settings, don't we Mr. Funk?"

The hospital bed seems to have engulfed my old man. He suddenly appears much smaller under his blanket and gown.

"Sorry, have we met?" Doctor Douchebag asks, wrapping a meaty hand around my fingers.

"I'm Isaac. Abe's kid."

"Oh yes, the one from out East. I heard Halifax will be joining Winnipeg soon in the new Canadian Premier League. You a soccer fan, Isaac?"

Doctor Douchebag seems oblivious to the fact that his particular brand of bedside manner won't work on me at all. The one and only time I've ever attended a sporting event was in grade four when Abe took me to see a Winnipeg Goldeyes game. Someone from the church offered him free tickets, so he couldn't refuse. I displayed zero interest in coming along until he sweetened the deal with the promise of a post-game trip to BDI for ice cream.

I actually had a good time, at least for the first hour. Goldie, the team's fuzzy yellow mascot, and perennial super fan Dancing Gabe kept the crowd entertained during breaks in play. Abe even splurged on a couple of hot dogs, which was unheard of. I was used to stuffing a package of Twizzlers down my pants whenever my old man splurged on a movie night at the cheap seats because I knew he didn't budget for snacks on top of tickets and gas. Maybe sports weren't so bad after all.

But one hour stretched into two, then three, then four and still the game was tied. Abe said we needed to stick around for overtime, or whatever they call it in baseball, but I was not having it. I started complaining, he snapped, and then we left to avoid any further social embarrassment. After all, as he sternly reminded me in the "outrageously priced" parking lot, there was every likelihood some of his congregation could have been in the crowd. And even if we weren't recognized, my antics "constituted a poor witness for all the other obedient children who were willing to enjoy the game in respectful silence with their parents."

Back in the car, Abe tuned into AM 670 for a live play-by-play and drove straight home to Newfield without the promised stop at BDI. I don't think he really cared about the game, but he'd made a commitment and we were going to honour it until the bitter end. We sat there in the driveway until it was dark, waiting for a change in score. I don't remember who won.

"You got lucky there with the leg, Mr. Funk," says Doctor Douchebag. "It was a nice clean break, so we didn't have to ship you off to Winnipeg. And the IV will help you get your fluids up. But I'm still concerned about your head."

I wince as the thud of skull on concrete echoes through my mind.

"Does he have a concussion?" I ask.

"It's possible. I'd like to keep him under observation for a while. And we might as well do OT and physio consults too. Won't be easy to get around the house. He'll need help. Unfortunately, we're a little short staffed at the moment, so it'll probably be tomorrow before they can see him."

"What about mental health supports?"

The manscaped brows pinch together in a frown. "What do you mean?"

"Well, are we sure this wasn't intentional? I understand he's currently on a leave of absence from work for depression."

"Isaac!" The old man pulls himself to a sitting position and glowers me into silence.

"Okay, so, let's just call a time out for a sec, shall we?" Doctor Douchebag takes a deep breath and pitches his voice up to a more chipper octave. "I'd like to stress that Mr. Funk's admission here is one hundred percent voluntary. As far as I'm aware, there is absolutely no indication that your father was trying to harm himself when he fell. Therefore, he is absolutely free to leave at any time. However, I am asking him to play it safe here and stick around just a bit longer. Are we clear?"

"As mud," I mutter.

"Now, Mr. Funk, you're going to be in some pain for the next few days and I'm going to write you a prescription for that. There's some increased risk of gastrointestinal bleeding when combined with your other medication, so I'd encourage you to go easy on these. But if you need some, take some. No need to be a tough guy here. Questions?"

I jump back in before Abe can speak. "Yes, actually. You're talking about antidepressants, right? That's the other medication Abe must be on. Because my doctor warned me about the stomach stuff when I was on them too. Just want to be clear, like you said."

"Isaac, that's enough," the old man says.

"Look I know this is uncomfortable, but you can't just keep all this inside. If you need help, just ask. You know I'm going to be around for at least a few months."

Abe pounds on his bed. "No! I wish to discuss this with my doctor in private. You and I can speak tomorrow, Isaac."

"But—"

"Please leave. Now."

I glare at my father and Doctor Douchebag, but neither man meets my eye.

"Fine!" I say. "Have it your way."

The hospital hallways all look the same. The only exit in my immediate vicinity is marked with a red sign that says WARNING! ALARM WILL SOUND IF PUSHED. I stalk past bulletin boards full of public health notices and community events. One has a tattered paper snowman stapled to the top. I wonder how long it's been up there. Maybe everyone's trying to ignore the thing until it makes sense again.

Outside, I want to Google Farthest Place From Winnipeg, but my phone informs me I'm out of data for the current billing cycle. I can't seem to find my parking ticket and all I want to do is turn the lot into my personal demolition derby. I take a deep breath. I suppose I should be happy Abe's staying the night here, if only to avoid me.

The ticket's in a pocket I'm sure I already checked. When the rusty arm finally swings up, I squeal the tires and gun it down to the Rouge to buy a case of Schlitz off Sandy. The stuff tastes like horse piss, but you could get a whole crowd "Schlitz-faced" back in high school just by pooling your loose change. I figure there's no need to break the bank for the pity party I have planned.

Muscle memory kicks in when I slide back behind the wheel of the Taurus. Reaching down under the passenger seat, I'm only half-surprised to find my old CD wallet still there. Oh Abe. Consider this a warning from the kettle to the pot. You really need to deal with your shit sometime. I replace the old man's Gaither Homecoming album with *Touch Up* by Mother Mother and skip ahead to track eight, my favourite. The music scours my brain like a Brillo Pad, loosening the day's mental grime until it begins to trickle away.

If you take St. Mary's Road a few klicks past Newfield, you'll soon reach an unassuming turnoff. It's just before a bridge that marks the place where the Red and Rat Rivers meet. The thin dirt track curling away from the highway is easy to miss if you don't know where to look, but I do.

When I get there, I park at the end of the rutted lane in a grassy field surrounded by a stand of scraggly trees, next to a faded wooden archway heralding the Mennonite Memorial Landing Site. If I wanted to, I could walk through that archway and down a path to the Red. I could stop along the way and read the stone cairn dedicated to the first Mennonite settlers who travelled here by steamboat nearly a hundred and fifty years ago before spreading across the Prairies like wildfire. Among them were my ancestors, those who displaced the land's Indigenous inhabitants to build a claustrophobic little paradise that became my holier-than-thou hometown.

The plaque in the woods phrases things a little differently, of course. Not that anyone ever stops by to read it. As much as we Mennos like to dwell on the past, no one in Newfield really wants to celebrate this part of our history. The awkward bit where we were penniless refugees and had to rely on the kindness of strangers.

Much better to focus on the present, where we're all healthy and wealthy and wise. These days there are Mennonite millionaires. Judges and cabinet ministers too. We've come a long way baby. Who's persecuting who now?

Anyway, all that to say there's really no reason to come here anymore, to the landing site. Not unless you want a quiet place to catch a catfish. Or host a bush party.

It came to me the summer after grade ten, on one of those hot restless nights. We kids wanted somewhere we could really let ourselves go. A party beyond our parents' reach. That's when I remembered this place, where Abe had once forced me to walk a mile in my ancestors' shoes.

The site was celebrating a big anniversary, and the elders of NMC decided that a historical re-enactment would be the best way to mark the occasion. Somehow, Abe pressganged me into playing one of the OG Mennolanders. Even borrowed costumes from the Mennonite Heritage Village, which were itchy and smelled of mildew.

The oldest living man in Newfield, Cornelius Duerksen, gave some long-winded speech about the rich blessing of growing up with an orange as his only Christmas present. Then after him, someone else got up and led us all in a hymn sing. I suppose the event took no more than an hour or two, but standing there under the hot sun in those heavy old clothes, I thought we might drone on like that for all eternity.

A lot can happen in a century and some change. I wonder what Newfield's founding fathers would have done if they'd found the remnants of bonfires and rusted beer cans left behind by me and my friends, our sins imprinted on the gummy clay shores of the Red River. The very spot where they once disembarked in pious anticipation was the same place where I first got black out drunk. Tried weed. Kissed my first girl. And boy.

I can feel my great-great-great-grandfather's hope hanging in the air here like mist. Hope that his people might finally perfect this experiment of intentional isolation for which they had suffered so greatly for so long at the hands of others. Hope that we, his descendants, might live free from tyranny in this new land. Well, the tyranny of others anyway.

A part of me wants to retrace their steps. Walk again in this place that marks the beginning and end of me in so many ways. Follow the river to somewhere new. Find my own promised land.

But the path down to the water is muddy. It'll be dark soon. There are swarms of mosquitos circling the car, waiting to mainline my veins. So I stay put and crack a beer instead.

What this town has done, it's like pickling people. Taking us when we're young and fresh and vulnerable, sticking us in a jar and filling us with all these rules they hope will preserve us from the rotting decay of worldliness. But you can't brine someone in that much guilt and shame their whole lives and expect them not to change. Shrivel into mere husks of their former selves, sour as vinegar.

The prairie sky is aflame with sunset, though dark clouds in the south threaten to douse the embers of the day. I watch as the summer storm stretches its arms over the horizon. Sheets of rain rush towards me. The car echoes with the pounding fists of the downpour. There's nothing to be done. I reach into the backseat for another Schlitz. Eventually, the torrential tantrum wears itself out.

14

I come to with a start, and the kink that's formed in my neck overnight screeches in protest. Ever so gently, I try to detach my sandpaper tongue from the roof of my mouth without tearing it in half. There's no water of course, just a dozen crushed cans of Schlitz littering the passenger seat. The air inside the car is thick with the scent of beer and my own BO. I get the door open just in time to hurl onto the wet grass.

Alrighty then. Let's go get the old man his holy book. And maybe a change of clothes for his son, the sinner.

I find Abe's bible inside a nightstand. In contrast to the bare and uncluttered house, his room is a total mess. The bed is unmade, its off-white sheets crumpled up like a used Kleenex. A jumble of hangers in the open closet stand vigil over a pile of dirty clothes. Every spare surface is covered with stacks of paper: sermon notes, receipts, old issues of the *Mennonite Brethren Herald*.

I was never allowed in here as a kid. Abe couldn't stand the thought of anyone knowing how he really lived. Still, I occasionally snuck in to ransack my mother's peeling vanity for any clues about her life. All the drawers were empty, but I liked to stare at my reflection in the cloudy mirror and imagine her getting ready for the day. Picking out earrings, combing her hair, putting on lipstick. Did she follow this routine on the day she left? Or did she slip away in the night with some hastily packed suitcase, weeping and dishevelled? Was it easy to go or did it eat at her heart? Did she tell her next lover about the family she left behind? About me?

A photograph slips out between the delicate pages of the old man's bible and flutters to the ground. I bend to pick it up, but nearly drop it again when I realize what I've found.

It's a photo of us: me, my mom, and Abe. The manmade lake behind us is instantly recognizable. I can taste the skunky brown water on my tongue, feel it lapping against my ankles like a puddle of lukewarm pee. St. Stache Provincial Park. No wonder I hated the beach before I moved to the ocean.

Though I have many memories of this place, none of them involve Loreena. In the picture I'm barely a toddler. We're sitting around a campfire, and she's got me on her lap. My face and hair are smeared with gooey streaks of marshmallow, chocolate, and graham cracker crumbs. There's a piece of paper towel in my mother's hand, but she's laughing too hard to clean up my face. Abe is reclining in a plastic lawn chair to our left, hands behind his head and the hint of a smile on his face as he takes in our struggle. We're so fucking happy it hurts.

NMC family campout, reads the neat note on the back, *Aug. '93*. I do not know this handwriting, so it must be hers. Surely this was from our last roll of film as a family, developed just a month before she left.

Abe has never shown this to me. He's not one to sentimentalize. Never bought the school picture package or hung a portrait of us on the wall. If it wasn't for the albums Opa Willie let me flip through, I wouldn't have known what Loreena looked like at all.

I stumble for the door, kicking a ratty shoebox and some twisted sweatpants out of my way. Why didn't he just burn this? If he'd destroyed it in a moment of anger I might have understood, but keeping this beautiful memory to himself all these years when he knew I wanted more? How could anyone be that cruel?

I toss my empties out of the car and plunk Abe's bible down in their place. It's time to pay my old man another visit. But I'm keeping the photo. If he wants it back, he'll have to ask me for it. And then I'll have some questions of my own.

A familiar floral stench wafts down the hall as I enter the St. Stache hospital, offering just enough warning for me to duck behind a large plastic plant. My aunt and uncle march by in their Sunday best. Their shoes click in unison across the tiled floor, the overhead fluorescents catching the gilded edges of their white leather bibles. Gina's perfume lingers in the air like mustard gas, but I manage to hold in my sneeze until they reach the exit.

I'm surprised to find Abe up and dressed when I reach his room. He's perched on the edge of his bed, folding some clothing into his overnight bag. A pair of crutches leans against the wall behind him.

"Going somewhere?" I ask.

He startles slightly, but quickly recovers. "Ah good, you're here. You can help me make the bed. I was having trouble reaching the far corner."

"I think they'll want to wash the sheets, actually."

"Oh," he says, offering an absentminded nod. "Of course."

"I brought this," I say, holding up his bible. "But it looks like you're ready to go home."

"Yes."

Abe fumbles with the buckle on his suitcase and attempts to stand, but he's off balance and lands back on the bed with a grunt.

"What's the rush?" I ask, exchanging the bag for his crutches.

"Someone might need the room."

"I thought that someone was you. Have you spoken with the occupational therapist?"

"No."

"Okay, what about physio?"

"They're busy people. I can take care of myself."

"Abe, you can barely walk. The doctor—"

"Said I'm free to leave whenever I wish," the old man retorts, straightening his spine.

I pause for a moment to collect myself. Try not to let him see me clenching and unclenching my fists.

"I know that, but I really think there should be a plan in place before we leave. Let's just wait a few more minutes until someone can come by and talk us through your options. I'll go check in at reception, see how long it might be."

Abe lurches to his feet and crutches towards the door. "My leg will be just as broken no matter where I am."

I toss the final conversational grenade in my arsenal to stop him. "Did Jake and Gina put you up to this? I saw them in the hallway."

My uncle has long been of the opinion that good health is all in the mind. He believes you can pray away any ailment with enough faith.

Abe hop-shuffles around to address me. "My brother was simply fulfilling his pastoral duties. He's taken over visitation for the church in my absence. I appreciated that he and Gina took the time to look in on me and uplift me in prayer. Now, if you don't mind, I'd like to have a rest in my own bed. There's no need to mope around here taking up space."

I raise my hands in surrender. "Okay, if that's what you really want."

"Thank you."

"You hungry at all?" I ask. "I can make us some lunch when we get back."

"That would be nice."

His eyes close for a moment as he exhales, lips parting in the thinnest shadow of a smile.

Abe can't stop staring at the fuel gauge the whole drive back to Newfield. He never lets the Taurus go below three-quarters full, but I haven't gassed up since yesterday and I can tell it's driving him nuts. I nudge the pedal a bit harder and watch him grimace with concern as the needle takes another dip. We hit half a tank at the *Welcome to Newfield* sign and Abe lets out a sharp wheeze of alarm like he's been stabbed.

"I was thinking of stopping in at the Co-op before we had home," I offer, trying not to laugh. "That okay with you?"

"If you'd like," he says, shoulders slumping with relief.

Pulling into pump one of two, we're instantly surrounded by a couple of teenaged attendants who come scurrying out from the gas station. One whips out a squeegee while the other stands at attention beside my open window.

"Fill with regular, please."

The girl nods and gets to work. Squeegee kid finishes up and offers to check the oil.

"Sure," I say, popping the hood for him. "Knock yourself out."

I feel bad for the kids who work here. I've never seen anybody tip at the Co-op before, even though the place offers full service come rain, shine, or a windchill of minus forty. The locals probably figure they shouldn't have to pay extra for something they could do themselves, even though they never do.

Squeegee kid presents the dipstick with all the panache of a world-class sommelier. I offer a nod of approval, though I have no idea what to look for. Behind him, the pump attendant patiently waits her turn to tell us the total. Damn these kids are good. Abe pulls out his wallet to pay, but I beat him to it.

"It's okay, I've got this."

I pass a few bills through the window, rattling off the old man's Co-op number by heart. The girl stares in slack-jawed disbelief when I tell her to keep the change, and I notice Abe's wearing a similar look.

"What? The Co-op number?"

He nods.

"I had to fill up here every time I borrowed the car in high school, remember?" I tap my temple as I pull out of the gas station. "Those six digits are locked in for all eternity."

When we get home, I give Abe an awkward hand out of the car. He mumbles something, possibly "thanks" or "ouch," before hobbling over to the house's side entrance. Inside, he heads straight for the recliner, plopping himself down with an extended old man groan. He sits there, panting heavily, and stares at the television's blank screen.

"Can I get you some water?" I ask, bringing over the remote.

He shakes his head no, but when I come in with a glass, he gulps it down in one go. I head back to the kitchen for a refill.

"Abe!" I raise my voice to be heard over the television. "When's the last time you went grocery shopping?"

There's absolutely nothing in his cupboards. No pasta, no canned soup, no salt and pepper shakers even.

"It's been a while," he calls back. "Check the garage."

There's an ancient freezer in the far corner of Abe's garage that hums like a swarm of killer bees. It's been entombed there since before my parents owned the house. I have to grip the faux wood handle with both hands and yank it at a diagonal to get it moving. The heavy lid creaks open like a vampire's coffin in some schlocky cartoon, but it's what I find inside that's truly horrifying.

There's not much to see. One pail of no-name plain vanilla ice cream. Two lumpy Ziploc bags whose freezer-burned contents are only identifiable as meat buns thanks to the elegant Sharpie label penned by some NMC bake sale volunteer. A stack of TV dinners takes up the rest of the space. Lord have mercy. Is this how he's been living since I moved out? Sure, I probably ate more than my fair share of takeout and frozen pizzas growing up, but Abe knew how to fire up the barbeque or make a sandwich back then. There were plenty of casseroles dropped off by my Aunt Gina and other well-meaning members of his congregation, and I added spaghetti and tacos into the mix after taking home ec in school. He's clearly let his cooking skills atrophy since those days, though.

This cannot stand. Oma Trudy would roll over in her grave if I fed her convalescing son a hunk of mystery meat zapped in the microwave. Only one meal will do in this situation, and that's sommaborscht. A soup shimmering with fat and flavour that Gina would ladle out whenever someone in the family was feeling under the weather or asked really nicely for a special treat. I've never made it myself, but with the miracle of modern technology, I find a recipe off some site called *Kitchen Kliewer* almost immediately.

"Give me your wallet," I say as I walk back into the living room, blocking Abe's view of the TV.

"Why?" He cranes his neck, trying to watch around me.

"Because I used up all my cash at the Co-op and I need to go to the store."

"I told you, there's food in the freezer."

"If that's your idea of food then I'll be praying for you, Brother Abraham."

I put my hand to my heart and give the old man my best look of sanctimonious pity. In response, his eyebrows lock into the infamous Unibrow of Disapproval, but eventually he reaches for his cash. I snatch the wallet from his hand and pluck out a couple of bills.

"If you're going to be running errands, you might as well pick up my new prescription and the, uh, refill too," he says. "The hospital faxed that over yesterday. Tell the pharmacist he can call me directly if there are any follow-up instructions."

"Sure thing."

"And nothing spicy please, I get acid reflux."

"Hold the flavour. Got it."

"Oh, and don't forget—"

"Receipt and change," I say over my shoulder. "I know the drill."

15

There's a shortcut you can take from the pharmacy to the grocery store if you don't mind reliving the trauma of your teen years while walking across some graves. I've always found it funny that Newfield's school was built right behind its only cemetery, children playing within spitting distance of all their dead relatives. Maybe that's just what it means to grow up Mennonite. No matter how brightly the sun might be shining, we're always living under the shadow of Judgement Day.

I spent twelve long years shuffling my gym bag and books down the same worn tiles of the school's only hallway, from the kindergarten classroom at one end to my grade twelve homeroom on the other. My worst nightmares still take place inside that building. Each time I'm transported through time to the mid-nineties. I'm stuck in my five-year-old body again, but somehow my adult memories are still intact. There's no way back to the present but to live through it all again, and so I do. Go to class. Learn my shapes and colours and the alphabet. Keep my head down. Make myself small. Day by week by month by year. Until I wake up.

I was on a first-name basis with everyone in my grade. We didn't have cliques exactly, just variations on the same theme. There were brownnoser Christians, rebellious Christians, Christian jocks and bullies and nerds. Atheism was not an option at a public school that started each day with the Lord's Prayer. In Mennoland, people think freedom of religion means Jesus lovers are free to shove their beliefs in your face. Every business on Main Street plays the local Christian music station on their sound systems. You can walk out of the credit union and into the café without missing the chorus of the same praise and worship song.

There was this game we used to play back in elementary school called Grounders. Everyone would scramble to the play structure during recess and the last one there was it. You had to close your eyes and wander around with your arms outstretched, feeling for someone to tag. Everyone else would scatter. Do their best to stay out of your way.

It was hard to catch someone outright when your eyes were closed. The best thing to do was keep moving, force people to leave their hiding spots. If you heard something, a crunch of gravel maybe, or the squeak of a hand letting go of the monkey bars, you'd shout "Grounders!" and anyone touching the ground would be it.

We kept playing that game for years, even after Kelvin Krahn broke his arm falling from the top of the fireman's pole while he was it and the teachers told us to stop. It was one of those rare cases where we actually dared to challenge authority outright. Everyone thought it was stupid to blame the game for the broken arm when it was obviously Kelvin's fault for not being more careful. Even Kelvin said that. Grounders *was* recess, and we weren't going to let anyone take that away from us. How else were we supposed to practise stepping out in blind faith?

It took me a while to realize how weird it all was. How different we were from the other kids we bumped up against during band trips and volleyball tournaments. Eventually though, I realized the rest of the world was actually Normalville. It was me who'd been living in Crazytown this whole time.

Even before I reach the cemetery, the ghosts are crowding in. That teacher who yanked the My Little Pony out of my hand during free play and replaced it with a Tonka truck. All the old friends who blocked my number the second their parents found out I was queer. Noah. Newfield won't let me forget. Even if the people all disappeared, I'm sure the stones would still cry out.

There's a scraggly patch of dandelions growing around the chain-link fence that separates playground from graveyard. I'm seized by a sudden urge to pick a couple for Opa. This would make him laugh. My grandfather spent any free time he had tramping around Wonder World with a canister of broadleaf herbicide strapped to his back, doing his best to eliminate the pops of yellow from his otherwise perfect lawn. No matter how much he sprayed, they always returned. He used to grumble about it, but secretly, I think he admired their tenacity. I even found a couple jars of dandelion wine the other week while helping Deb clear out the farmhouse cellar. I wanted to sample some, but there was no date on them, and Deb said she couldn't be a hundred percent sure they weren't laced with weed killer. Maybe I should bring a jar here and pour one out for Opa.

The fresh mound of dirt is right where I expect it to be, off in the northeast corner of the cemetery. The names *William Funk* and *Gertrude Funk* are encircled by roses intertwined with wheat sheaves. Four final numbers have been freshly cut into the granite. I once told Opa how creepy I thought it was to have a joint headstone just sitting here waiting for him to die, but he laughed it off.

"You think I'd pass on a two-for-one deal, jung? Besides, it gives me peace to know my name is there next to Trudy's. One day we'll be together again. In glory."

"Hi Opa," I whisper, kneeling before his grave. "It's me, Isaac. I just wanted to say thank you. For the farm? Also, I'm really sorry for being such a shitty grandkid. I should have called or flown out once in a while. I hope you understood why I didn't. But you figured out how to get me here in the end, didn't you? I've been thinking about Wonder World a lot since I got back. You made it so good for so many people. I want to find my own way to do that too. Something that would make you proud and—"

A harsh droning noise slices through the air, disturbing the moment. I look up to find a man in an orange vest advancing on my spot with a lawnmower.

Jesus Christ. Can't this stupid town give me one minute alone with my grandfather's corpse? I guess not. Nothing's ever private here. Especially not grief. I let the dandelions fall from my hand as I stand up. The mower will be here soon enough to turn them into mulch.

In the grocery store, I grab a cart and run through my list. Green onions and dill. Bag of boiling potatoes. Cream. I have no idea where to source the sorrel this recipe calls for, except that it definitely isn't this store. No luck on beet greens either. *Kitchen Kliewer* does recommend one final substitute, albeit with a disclaimer: *Though your Oma might not approve, spinach will do in an absolute pinch.* I toss a sad bag of wilted leaves into my cart and offer up a quiet apology to Oma Trudy.

I check off salt and pepper from the spices section and grab a package of farmer sausage from the meat cooler. Heading back to the checkout, I nod and smile at several people I know I am vaguely related to, though I can't remember how.

Neth spots me from her checkout lane and waves me over. Before I can respond, Gina glides out of a side aisle and blocks my path.

"*Isaac!*" she croons. "I was *hoping* we might *bump* into each other today. Doing some shopping for your father? What a *godsend* you are."

"Auntie."

She glances at the prescription bag in my cart and her teeth flash like high beams. "I heard your father's agreed to give *medication* another go. *Bless* him."

Nothing gets by this woman.

"I know he's not exactly the *easiest* man to be around when he's in one of his blue moods," she continues, "but I can't *tell* you how *relieved* Jacob and I both were when we heard you'd be looking in on him. And we want you to know we're here to support you *every* step of the way. It takes a *village*, doesn't it?"

"I should probably get back to him, actually."

Gina reaches out to clasp my hand, each cobalt blue nail a tiny dagger pressing deep into my skin. "Of *course,* dear, of course!" she says without releasing me. "You're a *busy* man. Oh! But before I forget, I wanted to invite you and Abraham over to our little abode for a wee *celebration* luncheon!"

"What are we celebrating?" I ask.

"Why, your return, your father's discharge, your grandfather's *generous* bequests, take your pick! I'm simply *dying* to hear all about your plans for the farm. Jacob mentioned the two of you had a little chat about it the other day. He's so *good* with that sort of thing. I didn't have a clue what to do after my own parents passed, but your uncle told me *exactly* where to invest and now we've *doubled* the inheritance! Or maybe it was tripled? Gosh, it's a good thing he has *such* a head for numbers, isn't it? We'd be simply *lost* without him."

Ah, so it's a business lunch she has in mind. Gina notices the expression on my face and quickly changes tacks.

"You know, William would be so *pleased* to see the whole family together again. His *greatest* wish was that we all might be reconciled someday. I was so blessed to have such a *godly* man for a father-in-law." She pauses to dab at her perfectly dry eyes. "Anyway, how does Saturday sound? Say one o'clock?"

"Sorry," I say, extracting my hand from her vicelike grip, "but Deb and I are going to be pretty busy on Saturday out at the market. All those city folks will be clamouring for our fresh veggies and relish to accompany their long weekend barbeques. We could have done Sunday lunch, except you and Uncle Jake have church. Abe doesn't, but I guess you know that already. So how about five o'clock Sunday? I'm sure the three of us will be free then."

Gina's face goes pale.

"*Three?*" she squeaks.

"Yeah, sure," I say. "Me, Abe, and Deb. Like you said, it'll be great to have *all* the Funks together again, right?"

Surely this will get her to back off. Deb hasn't been over for a family dinner in ages. Unfortunately, I seem to have underestimated Gina's resolve.

"*Certainly*," she says, knuckles whitening around her cart. "Five on Sunday it is. Now, if you'll excuse me, *Nephew*, I really must be going. *So* much to do."

"Of course, Auntie," I say, offering my sweetest smile. "See you Sunday."

Looking forward to the fireworks.

"She saw you come in," Neth tells me with a mischievous grin when I reach her checkout. "I watched her examine the same can of beans for ten minutes while she waited for you to finish your shopping."

"Fuck," I say. "I can't believe I just agreed to that. Deb's going to kill me."

"Sounds like you could use a night off from the fam. Wanna come over tonight?"

"Really? That would be amazing! I'll let you know when I'm done at my old man's."

"Great!" Neth says before lowering her voice. "Now if you'll excuse me, it appears the lovely gentleman behind you would like to pay for his kielke and onions with a shit tonne of loose change, so I'm going to need to free up some counting space."

Slice, boil, stir, taste. The calming rhythm of sommaborscht seems to come naturally to me. When it's ready, I call Abe to the table. His nostrils flare in pleasant surprise as he crutches in from the living room.

"Did you make—?"

"Oba jo! Sommaborscht!" I exclaim, filling two bowls with soup and finishing them off with a generous dollop of cream. "I didn't make buns or anything. But I can get some tomorrow for the leftovers if you want."

"Leftovers? Can't imagine there'll be any," Abe chortles, plunging his spoon into the broth with gusto.

"How is it?" I will the meal to taste as good as my aunt's.

"It's fine. Just fine."

That's as close to a compliment as I'm likely to get out of the old man, so I take it. We slurp in silence like a couple of monks until our bowls are empty.

"So I ran into Gina at the grocery store," I say casually as I put my dishes in the sink.

"Oh?"

Abe pushes his bowl towards me, indicating he'd like seconds.

"She wants us to come for supper on Sunday," I say, ladling out more soup.

"Hmm."

"I told her I'd invite Deb as well."

"I see."

Does nothing faze this guy? He's got to know how rare it is for his brother and sister to sit down in the same room. The old man and I have a lively conversation about this news in my head while I wait for him to down his second bowl of sommaborscht. It's a little bit of make-believe I used to do as a kid to deal with the crushing quiet at the dinner table every night. The real Abe doesn't even thank me for the meal. Instead, when he's finished, he simply sets down his spoon and asks what's for dessert.

Annoyed, I scrape back my chair and stalk into the garage, returning with the pail of plain vanilla I noticed earlier. A thick layer of ice crystals has formed over top of the ice cream and I have no idea how much is salvageable. I can practically hear Oma Trudy's disappointed sigh.

"Here."

I set the container in front of Abe with a bit more force than strictly necessary. After a futile search through his cutlery drawer, I slam it shut.

"Where's your ice cream scoop?" I ask.

He shrugs. "Don't have one."

I'd forgotten this particular quirk about the old man. All of his teaspoons are bent because he prefers to chip tiny slivers of ice cream out of the tub instead of using a bowl like a normal person. He likes to work his way from the edges to the centre in an even, circular pattern so as to maintain a level surface at all times. I can only imagine how long this particular pail has lasted without a hungry teenager in the house to disrupt his little ritual.

Next time I cook for him I'm bringing over a premium carton of French vanilla with some of Deb's rhubarb sauce to pour over top. I've become absolutely addicted to the stuff since I moved back. She and her Triple L friends make up a fresh batch every year and it's one of our best sellers at the farmer's market. Has Abe ever tasted it? I hope so. A life without rhubarb sauce is a sad life indeed.

After dinner, the old man watches more TV while I clean up the kitchen. I finally force him to leave the living room at nine o'clock and get ready for bed because apparently I am his parent now. He wants to do everything himself, but I have to step in when the cast gets tangled up in his pajama pants and he nearly does a faceplant. I catch him before he can bruise anything other than his ego and grab a kitchen chair for him to sit in while I finish getting him dressed.

"I'm going to head out now, but call me if you need anything, okay?" I say as I help him into bed.

He turns slowly onto his side, mumbling an incoherent response into his pillow.

"I've turned my ringer on," I press. "It's no trouble."

"Najo."

I give his shoulder a squeeze. "Good night."

"Yes," he says. "Okay."

As soon as I arrive at Neth's place, Connor stomps past me to his truck and squeals out of the driveway.

"What's his problem?" I ask as she hands me one of his beers from the fridge.

"Oh, he's just worried you've come back to sweep me off my feet. Or him."

Beer shoots through my nose and I wipe it away with the back of my hand. In gym class, Connor used to refuse to change until I was finished. If he ever saw me in one of the school bathrooms he'd turn around and walk out. The dude seemed to live in perpetual terror that I was some kind of man-eating Medusa, capable of turning him queer with just one look.

"God, he hasn't changed a bit since high school, has he? Guess I'll always be a greedy bisexual to him. He just can't fathom being friends with a girl he doesn't want to fuck, eh?"

Neth winces.

"Sorry," I say, "I didn't mean—"

"No, no," she says with a sigh. "You're not wrong. Having kids definitely forced me to grow up, but I'm not so sure about Connor. Anyway, let's forget about him. I want to hear about you."

I tell her about Abe's broken leg and my worries about his depression. "It's just going to be such a shit show when we go to that dinner at Jake and Gina's. Nobody saying what they really mean, everyone pretending to have a good time when they're secretly miserable. I just wish Abe would open up about how he's doing."

Sitting cross-legged on Neth's couch, I knead away at the knots in her neck while she stretches out below me.

"Okay, but try to see it from his perspective," she says. "Who exactly is he supposed to talk to? His brother who has the power to get him fired, or the son who's only just come back into his life?"

"Why is it always on me to make the first move?" I protest. "Why can't he make an effort for once?"

Neth holds up her palms. "I know, I know. This isn't all on you. But what I'm saying is, with something sensitive like this, it makes sense your dad wouldn't—ouch!"

"Sorry!" I say, realizing my fingers are digging into her shoulders. "You were saying?"

Neth leans forward and asks me to put some pressure on her lower back. I place my feet above her hips and make little movements with my toes like I'm treading water. She takes a few deep breaths before speaking.

"I don't think I've ever told you, but I had pretty bad postpartum depression with both of my kids. The first time I tried to deal with it on my own, but the second time I made the mistake of telling my mom. She took me to 'counselling,' which turned out to be a super awkward conversation in my great-uncle's rec room while Mom and my great-aunt made small talk and squares upstairs."

I let out a groan. "The Sommerfeld bishop?"

"That's the one! You can imagine how it went. He told me good Mennonites don't believe in psychology because they have faith. That I should read my bible and serve my family and let the joy of the Lord be my strength."

"I'm so sorry, Neth. That's bullshit."

"Yeah, it was. I hadn't had a full night's sleep in months and Connor was doing fuck all like always and I couldn't see a way out of this hell that didn't involve driving my minivan into the Red or swallowing all the pills in our medicine cabinet. And then here comes my family to hit me with the 'be a better Christian' guilt trip. It was real rough there for a bit."

I reach down and wrap my arms around my friend. "Oh Chicky, I had no idea. I'm so glad you're still here."

"Thanks," she says. "Me too. Luckily, I didn't listen to that asshole and found myself a support group in the city instead. Got my mom to babysit by telling her I was visiting a sick friend in the hospital."

"She never got suspicious?"

Neth shrugs. "She asked me once what had happened with my friend, and I told her the truth. That she got the care she needed, and she got better."

"So you're saying I should give Abe some space and let him figure this out on his own?" I ask.

"No, I'm saying if you want to be there for him just try not to be pushy about it. So many people want him to put on a happy face right now. You've got to show him it's safe to take off his mask around you. That you're willing to listen without trying to fix."

A sudden wailing from down the hall interrupts us.

"Goddammit! I keep telling Connor not to put on *The Walking Dead* until he's sure they're in bed."

Sure enough, a pajama-clad six-year-old enters the room a moment later and collapses into Neth's arms, howling about zombies.

"This could take a while," she whispers over her shoulder as she comforts her kid. "Maybe we could hang out again on the weekend?"

I extract myself with a sympathetic nod and head out to the Taurus. In a rare moment of magnanimity, Abe offered to let me hold onto the keys while I'm helping him out.

Back at the farmhouse, Dupps is asleep on my pillow. He grumbles as I shift him over a little to give myself enough space to lie down. My conversation with Neth about her depression keeps replaying in my head. When the awful thought grips me, I tell myself to stop being so ridiculous and go to sleep. A minute later, though, I'm fumbling in the dark for my clothes and the keys and careening into town.

Pulling into Abe's driveway, I try to calm my pounding heart and tiptoe towards his room. I watch his chest rise and fall with an even, steady rhythm for a good long while. He doesn't appear to be in any kind of distress. The old man stirs in his sleep, then settles. I suddenly realize how weird it would be for him to wake up and find me here, standing over him. Still, I check his medicine cabinet and count all his pills before I leave, putting the tallies into my phone to help me keep track of what he is taking and how fast he's taking it.

This is me, not talking about it. I'm a good Mennonite.

16

"**Absolutely not.** Are you out of your damn mind?"

I'm starting to realize waiting until the day before the dinner to tell Deb about Gina's invite was a bad idea. Jam jars chatter and quake as she slams a crate of veggies onto our market table. At least we're sold out of eggs. One less thing she can pelt me with.

"Look, I'm sorry, okay?" I plead. "But this is obviously an excuse to get me and Jake together again so he can pressure me to sell the farm. I could really use your help here."

Deb turns away from me, not to cry, but to light a cigarette. A fashionable couple dragging along a trembling pair of whippets veers away from us and moves along to another stall. Deb blows some smoke and steadies her breathing before responding.

"You're really something, you know that?" she says. "Couple of days ago you're chewing me out for doing repairs on the property, and now you're acting like we're business partners. I told you before, kid. What you do with the farm is your decision. I spent my whole damn life looking after that land while my brother plotted out how to parcel it off to the highest bidder. If you don't want to talk to Jake, then don't. But don't drag me into this."

"You're right," I say. "This is my problem. And I'm trying to come up with a solution. I know how much you and Opa loved Wonder World. I loved it too. I don't want to see it bulldozed. I just need some time to figure this out. Please come with me tomorrow. I need you. You know how to handle Jake better than anyone."

Deb tosses her cigarette onto the gravel and crushes it with her boot.

"You want to know the truth, Isaac? Jake and I haven't been in the same room in five years. That petty asshole abused his wife's position to keep me out of Sunset Villa. They stole my last few years with Dad, and I'll never forgive them for that. I know it was hard for you to come back here, but you're not the only one who's struggling. This is something you'll have to figure out on your own. I've got to get back to the truck. We're running low on zuke relish."

I call after her, but she doesn't stop walking. A hesitant group of shoppers mill about, waiting to pay me. There's no following her. I put on my customer service smile and turn to the nearest person.

"How can I help you?"

As usual, the television is on at Abe's place when I arrive on Sunday afternoon to pick him up for the big dinner. I recognize the theme song to a local televangelism program called *Sermons for the Shut-Ins*. The show's raspy-voiced host, the Reverend Doctor Horace J. Blatherly, has been renting airtime across the Prairies for the better part of two millennia. Each week, he squeezes two hymns and a vaguely judgemental sermon decrying the immoral excess of our age in between syrupy donation appeals to fund his private jet or some equally essential tool of evangelism. As the name of the show implies, his primary audience is anyone aged fifty to a hundred and fifty who doesn't get out much but still holds a valid credit card.

"Hey Abe! It's me. Are you ready to go?"

Blatherly is playing to an empty living room. I turn off the TV and call again for the old man but get no reply. No one's in the bathroom either. A sense of unease twinges somewhere behind my left ear just before I enter Abe's bedroom. I pause for a moment, feeling my pulse in my throat as I rest a hand on his door.

I'm sure he's okay. But what if he's not?

I knock and push myself forward. The old man is in bed. He's staring up at the ceiling and still in his pajamas, but at least he's breathing.

"Uh, hi. How's it going?" I ask.

Abe blinks once, twice, three times.

"Fine. Thank. You."

He takes a long, slow breath between each word.

"Really? Because you seem kind of ..." Gloomy? Catatonic? Pitiful? "Tired. Did you sleep okay last night?"

"Yes," he wheezes.

"Do you need help with anything? Getting dressed? Going to the bathroom?"

"I can. Manage."

Every word seems to be an effort to get out. Each time he blinks, it seems like his eyes stay closed for a fraction of a second longer. When he finally does open them again, his gaze is distant.

"I was just engaging. In some. Quiet. Reflection," he says.

"Yeah? About what?"

"Family."

Do we care to expand on that? I give him a moment. Nope, we do not.

"You took your pills today?" I ask, concerned.

"Yes."

"How many?"

"The right. Amount. They make me. Tired."

This isn't exactly unexpected. I read the wad of warnings that came with his antidepressants. They were printed on tissue paper intricately folded into some sad origami. Turns out there's still a lot of trial and error involved in jumpstarting a brain. What helps one person might hurt another. The list of possible side effects was as long as my arm, and very contradictory. Drowsiness is common, but so is insomnia. Abe might experience diarrhea or constipation, increased nausea or a bigger appetite. Blurry vision, seizures, and vomiting blood are rare but not unheard of. A small number of patients can actually experience an *increase* in suicidal thoughts during their first few weeks on the drug. If this happens, you're advised to contact your doctor immediately, but how can I trust my father to do that when even on a good day he struggles to articulate what he wants for breakfast?

I go over to the window and open the curtain a crack. "How are you feeling about supper tonight?"

The old man squeezes his eyes shut and lets out a big sigh. "Isaac, was I a bad father?"

This sudden question catches me completely off guard. How do I answer that one?

Gee, Abraham, let's see. You've been emotionally distant since I was a small child, you threw me out of the house for kissing another boy, and then you didn't speak to me for ten years. If you're holding out for a #1 Dad mug, you might have to wait some time.

"I think you did the best you could."

The words surprise me as they come out of my mouth, but they're not untrue. I've had plenty of time to work through my anger about the way things went down between us, but looking down at this fragile body before me, all I feel is sadness. Like Deb said, I'm not the only one who's got problems. Maybe it's time to put aside this policy of Mutually Assured Desolation and make the first move.

Abe's face softens a little at my response. "It was hard. For me. When your mother walked away."

"Me too," I say.

"I thought. She could be. Happy with me," he murmurs as his eyes cloud over. "But the world. She wanted was. Bigger. Than I could offer."

There's a shoebox twisted up in his sheets, the same one I tripped on while looking for his bible the other day. An old photo, curled at the edges, lies on top. I recognize this as the post-skydiving image Abe described to me the other day. It's true Loreena does look incredibly happy. The way the shot is framed, she also looks completely alone.

I reach for the photo, but Abe puts his hand out to stop me like it's a hot stove.

"Would you like to reschedule tonight and stay in?" I ask. "I'm sure Jake and Gina won't mind."

I mean, they'll be livid, but who cares? A rain cheque would give me the chance to look after the old man and maybe patch things up with Deb too. The only thing she's said to me since yesterday's market was "Coffee's in the pot."

"I will go," Abe moans, on the verge of tears.

"I don't think that's a good idea. I'm going to call Gina."

"No!" he grips my hand with a fierce determination. "Family is important. I just need a. Moment. Please. To clear my head. Then I will get ready."

"Are you sure that's what you want?"

"Yes."

I stare my old man down, trying to summon the energy to fight him on this. But it's his life. A night out with my aunt and uncle isn't my idea of a good time, but perhaps it's encouraging that he wants to be with other people right now.

"Alright then," I say, carefully extricating my hand from his. "I'll be right outside if you need me. And we can always come back early if you start feeling tired again."

"Thank you," he pants, straining to raise himself into a sitting position. "Yes. Thank you."

"And Abe?" I say, pausing at the door. "You weren't the perfect parent, but you are the one who stayed. I think that's why it hurt so much when you pushed me away."

The old man turns his face to the window. Though he squeezes his eyes tight, a single tear still manages to escape.

What a shit show tonight's going to be. Deb, I don't know how I'm going to make it through this without you.

17

Abe and I are fifteen minutes late for dinner. I roll up to my aunt and uncle's long horseshoe driveway and park as close as I can to the front door. Their ranch-style compound sprawls across a double lot on the southwest edge of town. The place is a stucco-sided monument to mindless consumerism, excessively extravagant in the most pointless of ways. Like, why do they need a four-car garage when there are only two of them?

I help Abe past gaudy Grecian columns to the French front doors. The doorbell chimes out what sounds like the opening bars of "Praise God, from Whom All Blessings Flow" when pressed.

"Oh, thank *goodness*," Gina exclaims as she flings open the doors. "The ham was *nearly* too dry to serve! *Please* come in. Welcome to our *humble* home."

Inside, the cavernous interior is fifty shades of beige. A wrought iron chandelier dangles from the ceiling, twisted into some avant-garde design that resembles a giant spider. There are massive photos of my aunt and uncle in gilded frames walking through autumnal landscapes with their hands in the back of each other's designer jeans as far as the eye can see. God. Must have cost them a fortune to make the place look this tacky.

"*Jacob* dear, our *guests* are here!"

My aunt's singsong voice and her bright, flower-patterned dress put me in mind of *The Stepford Wives*. Every available ledge holds a puddling array of lit candles in thick glass jars that bombard us with a cacophony of competing scents: sandalwood, lilac, citrus, pine. Gina guides us over to an ornate bench and pulls out a wicker basket full of hand-knit slippers.

"If you don't mind, we've just had the *hardwood* redone. Wouldn't want to *scuff* it."

And here I was planning to walk around in my razor blade-studded socks like an idiot.

Mayor Jake breezes into the room wearing an expensive looking suit. He shakes our hands with the same seesawing motion I'm sure he's employed at countless rubber chicken dinners. His grip is inescapable until he chooses to let go.

"Abe! Isaac! Good to see you, good to see you. Glad we were able to set this up. But we were expecting one more, weren't we?"

"Unfortunately, Deb is feeling under the weather," I say. "She sends her regrets."

The mayor and my aunt exchange a look of gleeful triumph.

"Is that so? What a *shame*," titters Gina. "I suppose I'll need to rearrange the dining room then. Why don't you boys make yourselves *comfortable* in the den for a few minutes and I'll let you know when everything's ready? Abraham, do you need a *stool* for your poor leg? Jacob, *make sure* your brother gets a stool."

"Of course, dear," my uncle says, nodding like a bobblehead.

Gina scuttles off while we finish de-shoeing. Abe and I slip and slide along the polished floors behind my uncle to a room full of enough overstuffed leather couches to accommodate the Blue Bombers' entire roster. There's no TV, but only because Jake's installed a home theatre projector screen that takes up an entire wall. We stare at a football game for a few minutes before Gina invites us into the dining room. It takes my uncle and I three tries to haul Abe up from his low-slung chair.

Jake ushers us to the dining room table, a mahogany monstrosity that must have required the destruction of a small tropical rainforest to make. Each of us has been assigned a place with a gold-edged name card written out in my aunt's elegant, flowing script.

Gina claps her hands. "Well then. So *nice* to have you both with us. Jake and I have been *really* looking forward to tonight, *haven't* we dear?"

"Of course, dear," my uncle echoes.

The flickering light of a thousand noxious candles casts expectant shadows over their faces.

"Now *Abraham*," Gina says, "would you be so *kind* as to say grace for us?"

"O-oh," stutters Abe, "I, uh ..."

Jake sees his opportunity and swoops in.

"That's alright brother, allow me. Heavenly father—"

Just then the peals of "Praise God, from Whom All Blessings Flow" echo through the house. The door slams, and Gina grimaces at the loud thunk of two heavy boots being tossed onto her recently refinished hardwood. Deb appears in the dining room doorway a second later.

"Sorry I'm late," she says. "I brought wine."

And indeed she has, a bottle of red the size of a stout toddler. Bless her.

Without waiting for instructions, Deb moves Abe's crutches aside and plunks a spare chair down between him and me.

"Debbie," the mayor says through his teeth, "What a surprise. We understood you would not be joining us tonight."

"Well, *Jakey*, turns out I am," Deb retorts, placing her elbows on the table. "Got any wine glasses, Gina? Guess I'll need a fork and a plate too."

Our hostess stares at Deb, her mouth opening and closing like a goldfish. Finally, her husband stands and steers her into the kitchen. Cupboard doors bang and dishes clank, muffling their frantic conversation.

"You look amazing!" I whisper.

Deb's wearing one of Opa Willie's vintage suits, a three-piece charcoal number with light grey pinstripes and a matching bow tie. The familiar scent of cinnamon, peppermint, and cloves emanates from the fabric. Opa used to douse himself in Schlagwasser at the end of every workday. The strong-smelling oil came in little brown bottles sold by a Paraguayan friend with "connections" who claimed it was a miracle cure for everything from stomach aches to sore joints. Though I used to poke fun at my grandfather's devotion to the folk remedy, inhaling it now makes me instantly calmer and more relaxed. It's like he's right here in the room with us.

My aunt winks at me. "Thanks kid. Wanted a bit of Dad with me tonight. How are you doing, Abe?"

The old man shrugs. "I'm here."

"Yep," Deb says with a laugh. "That about sums it up, doesn't it?"

I reach out to grab her hand. "I know this isn't easy for you. It means a lot to me that you came."

"Tell you what," she says, squeezing back. "I'm going to need a long smoke after this, so why don't you buy my next pack, and we'll call it even?"

"You got it."

Our hosts re-emerge all smiles. Gina places a crinkled name card stained with grease in front of her sister-in-law before filling the table with platters and platters of food. Mayor Jake sets out goblets of cut crystal for Deb's bargain booze, though he and Gina stick to sparkling water. Conversation starts and sputters a few times over the screech of cutlery on plates. No one seems in the mood for small talk.

"Isaac," Jake eventually says, "I suppose this must be your first time celebrating Homesteader Day in a while. Any particular plans?"

My uncle has entertained some pretty harebrained projects as mayor. Like when St. Stache was digging out their lake in the eighties, he convinced them to dump all the excess dirt in Wilhelm Park so he could bill Newfield as "home of the largest manmade sliding hill in Manitoba." Unsurprisingly, toboggan tourism isn't a thing. Townsfolk have been stuck with a lumpy eyesore in place of their soccer field ever since.

Then there was the time he decided to rename our streets after Newfield's founding fathers. The mayor appointed a committee of local historians to make some recommendations, but he didn't account for the shallow nature of our town's shared gene pool. In the end, everyone agreed that while First, Second, and Third Street weren't very exciting, they were far more sensible options than A. Friesen, B. Friesen, and C. Friesen Way.

Considering his track record, Homesteader Day is definitely one of my uncle's less dumb ideas. For the past twenty years, Newfield has shut down Main Street on the first Monday in August for an old-timey fair honouring our pioneering ancestors. A flatbed trailer is hauled onto the school parking lot and transformed into a stage for local country and gospel bands. There are fireworks and free food and a knipsbrat tournament in the church basement that Opa won every year I can remember. It's a little hokey, but the most fun the elders will let us have. It also keeps people here on the long weekend, which means they end up spending more money at local businesses. Certainly makes the mayor's major donors happy.

"I don't know," I say. "I'll probably hang out with my friend and her kids."

"Well, be sure to stop by the town's booth," Jake says. "My office girls are in charge of the rollkuchen and watermelon this year and we've got some great swag to hand out with the town's new slogan on it."

"What's that?" I ask.

"'Newfield: A Good Place To Grow.' Catchy, isn't it?"

"Uh, sure. I guess."

"Of course," he continues, "I would've loved to announce the plans for Riverview Terrace at this year's festivities, but I don't want to rush you. Maybe next year we can do a ribbon cutting ceremony with the first show home."

"That sounds like an *excellent* idea!" says Gina. "We'll get you and Isaac a *big pair* of golden scissors!"

I force a smile as I set down my fork. "As I said the other day at the town office, I'm not quite sold on these development plans. In fact, the more I hear about Riverview Terrace, the less I like it. I was hoping you'd invited us here tonight to share a family meal, but if you're that anxious to talk business, let's do it. I don't think I'm going to sell the land after all, and certainly not to you. Now, shall we move onto dessert?"

"How *dare* you take that tone with us!"

"Now, now my dear," the mayor says, patting his blustering spouse's hand. "I told you our nephew had ambition. He's simply testing the waters to see how high the price will go, isn't that right, Isaac?"

I shake my head. "This isn't about money."

"That's rarely true in my experience," my uncle says with a chuckle. "You know, the thing about gambling, Nephew, is that it only works if you know when to cash in. Real estate is a tricky business. If you're looking to spark a bidding war, I should warn you there are very few people in this province who could compete with my investors. They can be very aggressive when they see an opportunity. Why go through all that trouble just to end up with our original offer at the end of the day?"

"You're not hearing me, Jake," I say, enjoying how he flinches at the use of his first name. "I said I don't want to sell. I want to keep the farm in the family."

"But what are *you* going to do with a property that size?" Gina asks. "You don't know the *first thing* about farming!"

"Well, as our esteemed mayor has reminded me, I need someplace where I belong. And the longer I'm here, the more I realize Wonder World is that place. Not just for me, but for everyone like me too."

"Like *what?*" scoffs Gina. "*Homosexuals?*"

I glance at Deb and can't help smiling. "That's right, Auntie.

Turns out the gay agenda is alive and well in Newfield, and I think it's time we got ourselves a new headquarters."

"Kid," Deb breathes, "what are you saying?"

"That a queer-friendly retreat centre is just what this town needs. And I could really use a partner to make the magic happen, if you can forgive me for being such a little shit the past few weeks."

"I knew *she* was behind this, Jacob. Didn't I *warn* you?"

The mayor slams his hand down onto the table, rattling the glassware. "This is ridiculous! You're just like that crazy mother of yours. Always got your head in the clouds. But I'm not going to let you stick my town with some slapdash rainbow-covered eyesore you abandon as soon as the going gets tough."

"Please," Abe whispers, the cloth napkin on his lap twisted into sweaty knots. "Don't fight."

"You think fear of bad press will keep me from contesting the will?" Jake asks, ignoring his brother's plea. "Gina and I have always said Dad's mind was failing him the last few years. I'm not convinced he could even read all the paperwork for that bogus will, let alone comprehend it. Probably a forged signature. With the right lawyers and experts backing me up, any judge is going to see things my way."

Abe sits up in his chair, meeting his brother's eye for the first time. "It won't work, Jake."

"Excuse me?" the mayor says, his voice quivering with rage.

"Dad's lawyer was very thorough. Everything was signed and dated and witnessed as it should be. H-he even had a psychological profile written up. Just in case. You may not like what he did, but Dad was certainly of sound mind when he did it, d-despite the rumours that someone was withholding medication and food from him at times. There are people who could testify to that."

Jake stares at his brother. Realization dawns. "You did this. You brought those people into the Villa. What did you tell the staff, that Pastor Abe was bringing some elders by for a bible study?"

Abe casts his gaze back down to his lap. "We have a lot of cousins, if you go back far enough. I told them the truth. That I had some family who wanted to see Dad. No one asked any questions."

"Well, there you go, Jake," Deb says, a smile playing across her face. "I guess your little scheme wasn't all that airtight after all."

Gina throws her napkin onto the table. "Abraham you *snake*. After all we've done for you, how could you *betray* us like this?"

"What do you mean 'all you've done?'" I ask. "Kicking him out of church because of his mental health? Isolating him from his community just like you did with Opa? Pushing him to reject me just for kissing another boy? You want everyone to see you as the model Christian couple, but all I see are two bitter, self-righteous hypocrites."

"And you think your *father* isn't?" Gina retorts, an angry blush blotching across her face and chest. "That he always has everyone's *best interests* at heart? Then tell me, *Nephew*, why did he hide those letters your *poor* mother sent you all those years ago? Why did he *prevent* the two of you from getting in touch again after she left? Yes, you heard me. Abraham Funk's no *saint*."

Everyone is standing and shouting at once, except for Abe and me. I can't feel the chair anymore, or the table. My ears fill with white noise. The stench of the candles and the ham and the Schlagwasser overwhelm my nose all at once, and the wine in my belly starts to swirl back up towards my mouth. Abe is all I can focus on.

"Is it true?" I ask him.

The tears in his eyes are the only confirmation he offers.

I can't keep the rage in any longer.

"Goddamn you, Abe. You had no right!"

"Isaac, please!" Deb pleads, gripping my arm. "It's complicated. He wasn't trying to hurt you."

"This fucking family!" I yell. "Everyone knew and no one told me? You people are all the same. I hate you."

Jake and Gina stand across from me with their arms folded, their faces identical masks of smug indifference.

"Kid."

I pull everything I'm feeling inside of me again. Make my voice cold and hard and small.

"No, Deb. I don't want to hear it. Where are the letters?"

"Shoebox," Abe mumbles through a thick, phlegmy throat.

Of course.

The keys to the Taurus are poking into my leg. I snatch the bottle of wine off the table. "Don't follow me," I spit out, reaching down to rip Gina's stupid slippers off my feet.

18

Everyone knows you've got to play it smart if you want to avoid the Night Watch. The volunteer group was Mayor Jake's response to our town's most recent "crime wave" in 2005, when a ride-on mower stored in an unlocked shed on the east side of town was mysteriously driven two and a half blocks west before being abandoned in a ditch. Rather than pay for extra patrols from the RCMP detachment in St. Stache, the mayor set up some citizen snitches with a second-hand cellphone, a Pontiac Montana on loan from the town office, and personalized travel mugs printed with their names and the Night Watch logo. Every weekend during the summer months, local busybodies patrol the streets of Newfield from dusk 'til dawn, their fingers just itching to call the cops' non-emergency line with reports of local hooliganism.

I ditch the Taurus at Abe's place after filling up a grocery bag with Deb's wine, Loreena's shoebox, and a few cans of warm beer left over from my drive out to the landing site. The last thing I need right now is to be interrogated by a cranky octogenarian hopped up on caffeine and adrenaline, and I know a parked car would paint an easy target on my back.

I set out on foot, trying first Wilhelm Park and then the school playground, leaving empty cans in my wake. Every time I think I've found the perfect hiding spot, a passing set of headlights makes me jump. I need somewhere I can be alone with Loreena's letters, but privacy's a tall order in Mennoland.

Neth and I used to be pretty good at scaling the school gym. There's an old drainpipe you can cram your fingers and shoes into so you can haul yourself all the way up to the roof. But that was a long time ago. I'm too out of shape and definitely too drunk to attempt that right now.

There's one other place I could go, but you'd have to be crazy to try it. Steph P., the waitress from Oma's Kitchen, used to talk about going there all the time. She was a notorious lightweight at our bush parties back in high school. Whenever she got loaded, she'd sing Hoobastank and Nickelback songs at the top of her lungs, French kiss anyone within reach, and then beg someone to stay up and watch the sunrise with her. Her mom was a production technician at Flatlander Feeds and Steph P. always claimed it was possible to hang out at the top of the feed mill on Sunday mornings when the place was closed.

"That sounds super dangerous," I said one time when she was trying to convince me to go with her.

"Well, sure, it's tall," she responded. "Probably a hundred and fifty feet, but that doesn't mean it's dangerous. There are stairs most of the way to the top. And once you're up there, you can see for miles and miles. It's totally worth the climb."

I decided to humour her with a few questions while my sweaty palm probed under her shirt. "But how would we even get inside?"

"There's an emergency exit that leads straight to the staircase," Steph P. whispered, nibbling my ear.

"Yeah, but even so. Wouldn't we need a key?"

"The lock's broken," she said.

I stopped kissing her. "You're shitting me."

"No, honest. My mom showed me. She said it's been that way for ages, and nobody's bothered to fix it."

"What about cameras?" I asked. "Alarm systems?"

Steph P. laughed. "Don't forget the booby traps and rabid

guard dogs," she joked. "I'm telling you, man, no one cares. It would be so easy."

She's not wrong. The door is around the back of the feed mill, hidden from Main Street. It squeaks open with a good push, and no sirens or flashing lights give me away. Even the nearby streetlight is burned out. There's no one standing guard. No one to watch me slip inside. Sometimes, small-town life has its perks.

The air inside the mill is tinged with a peaty funk, like someone tossed dog food into a popcorn machine. I walk down an echoey concrete hallway to a large room full of conveyor belts and mixing machines. Red lights blink ominously in the dark, but all is quiet as I make my way towards the long metal staircase at the back. Chips of paint slough off in my hand as I reach for the rusty railing. A little souvenir from the chillest B&E in history.

"See? Easy," I whisper, trying to calm my racing heart.

My legs are already shaking by the time I reach the top of the staircase. There's an access hatch that must lead to the roof. I crack it open, and clean, cool air rushes in.

Success!

I step into the softening gloom and take in my new surroundings. A mistake.

I am much, much higher up than I expected. Gazing down at the ground far below, my head starts to spin. There's only one way forward, a rickety ladder surrounded by a tight safety cage stretching up into the night. I clutch the bag and take a few deep breaths. I've found my quiet place. The Night Watch will never think to look for me up here, and my phone is turned off, so Abe and Deb can't bother me either. They've kept Loreena's words from me for more than twenty years, but not anymore. I place my foot on the ladder's bottom rung, squeeze my way into the cage, and start my ascent.

It's slow going with the grocery bag looped around my wrist. The wind rattles the bars around me like a child taunting a lion in the zoo. A cowardly lion in this case. I keep my eyes on the rung in front of me as I inch upwards. Once or twice I have to pause. Shake out my cramping hands. Calm my trembling limbs. At least the adrenaline and the cold breeze seem to have siphoned some of the booze out of my brain.

Finally, I emerge from the top of the cage onto Newfield's highest point, a narrow platform with perhaps three feet of space between the ladder and a large auger. I raise my fists in silent triumph, King of all Mennoland.

The beers are gone. I take one last swig of wine and toss the rest over the side. The bottle smashes on the parking lot far below, staining the gravel a darker shade of black.

"Here's to you, Loreena."

As a kid, I figured it had to be my fault she'd left town. Maybe I disturbed the delicate equilibrium that kept my parents in each other's orbit. Maybe I was such a terrible baby that my mother had no choice but to leave. I had to be unlovable somehow. Why else would she abandon me without saying goodbye?

Now, it seems I have my answer. She didn't let me go. Not fully. The old man kept her from me.

The wind picks up again. I hunker down and hug the shoebox close. With shivering fingers, I carefully crack the lid and peer inside.

My heart sinks as I take in the meagre contents of the box. Gina was wrong. There aren't any letters, just a handful of aging postcards. *Beautiful Banff. Greetings from the Grand Canyon. The Sun's Always Shining in Puerto Vallarta.* They're all addressed to me, but the hastily written notes on the back contain no useful information. Her comments are vague and banal, the kind of sentiments you might express to a prudish aunt who helped finance your travels. There's no *Call me when you're older* or *I hope someday you'll understand.* After a few months, the postcards stop.

At the bottom of the box there's a single envelope. It's worn at the edges, as if someone has held it many times. The envelope contains a third birthday card. Nothing special, just a cheap dollar store find with a droopy clown on the front. Inside there's a single sentence, the last one Loreena ever wrote me:

Happy birthday my beautiful boy, be well.—Mom

There's no return address. Must have been an oversight on her part. There were so many important things to do that day.

1. Lounge around on the beach, making sure to get an even tan.
2. Ask the front desk for use of their fax machine to send divorce papers back to devastated ex.
3. Buy yourself a new—

No.

I can't do this.

It hurts too much.

The platform is buffeted by a violent gust. I cling to the railing as the whole structure shudders. The wind tugs at the shoebox. At first I tighten my grip, but then it hits me. I don't need to hold onto this stuff. It won't tell me what I really want to know. There's no easy explanation here. Loreena stopped looking back a long time ago. Now it's my turn to move on.

I let the breeze take the box. My last tenuous connections to the woman who birthed me scatter in every direction and disappear into the night.

I don't know how long I stay crouched on that little platform, crying into the wind. The sun, when it rises, is indeed beautiful. A thin band of light creeping up along the horizon, eating away at the dark. It's a cloudless dawn, the air stretching thin and clear over the dome of the world as day is flicked on, drenching everything in shades of pink, orange, gold. It's nauseating.

Below me, Newfield is waking up. A convoy of brightly coloured semis rumbles into town, hauling carnival games and rides destined for the Homesteader Day midway. An ambulance sails by, lights on but sirens silenced. SUVs and half-tonnes fill the parking lot across the street at Oma's Kitchen. Men meeting other men for coffee like they have for twenty, fifty years. Life goes on.

All at once I am very hungry and very tired. I never grabbed my pay from Deb after the market on Saturday, so the café's famous farmer sausage omelette will have to wait for another day. I shimmy down the ladder and slip out of the feed mill. Walking down Main Street, I watch as some carnies transform a flatbed into a Ferris wheel. Why do we pay money to sit on such delicate metal seats designed to come apart at a moment's notice?

The nostalgia is hitting hard. Homesteader Day used to be the highlight of my summer. To me and Neth it represented a rare taste of freedom, a chance to day drink and goof around while all the adults were off volunteering at the food booths and main stage. In the evening, Opa would pick us up from wherever we were and drive out to one of his fields with blankets and hot chocolate so we could watch the fireworks together from the bed of his truck. If he noticed us slipping some smuggled Kahlua or Baileys into our enamel camping mugs, he never let on.

I should swing by Abe's place. Apologize for flipping out yesterday. Sure, he kept Loreena's notes from me, but maybe I would've done the same in his shoes. There were never any answers in that box, just old wounds waiting to reopen. Still, I had a right to know the truth, even if it wasn't pretty. I need some time to sit with all that I'm feeling. The old man's not going anywhere. Today, I just want to be a kid again.

There's only one place left to go, so I go there. Knock and stand outside, waiting.

"Hi," I say when the front door opens. "Can I come in?"

19

Neth offers me a fresh cup of coffee when I rouse myself
from her couch a few hours later. We set up two fraying lawn
chairs in the shade of her open garage and keep an eye on her kids
at the end of the driveway. They wanted to be in position with
their pillowcases nice and early. It isn't every day in Mennoland
that candy rains from the sky.

Soon enough, the first tractor trundles by, followed by a
combine and a grain truck. The kids whoop with excitement,
and pump their arms in the air, pleading for blasts from every
horn. I don't know whose idea it was to drive a convoy of farm
machinery through town every year on Homesteader Day, but
everyone agrees that the candy throwing makes it a parade.
The procession gradually winds its way along every single street
in Newfield, so there's no need to leave your house to join
in the fun.

"Breakfast?" Neth asks, tossing a bag of dill pickle knacksot
my way.

I laugh and scoop up a heap of the seasoned sunflower seeds.
"Where's Connor?"

"Dunno," she says. "Haven't seen him since he stormed out on
Thursday night."

"That happen a lot?"

"What do you think?"

Neth takes the bag back and pops some sot into her mouth. Cracks shells with her teeth. Spits.

"Everyone said all our problems would work out so long as we got married," she says. "The elders were a bit reluctant to let us have a church wedding what with my 'condition,' but mom convinced them in the end. I think your dad helped out with that too. It was so weird having him there but not you. Always thought you'd be my man of honour."

"I know, Chicky. Me too."

"The pictures were awful. It was thirty-five degrees out and my dress was this polyester monstrosity on sale from MCC. I got a heat rash right away, and my hair kept drooping to the side no matter how many cans of hairspray they doused me with. Nobody's smiling. I never got them printed."

The parade continues to inch along. Neth's kids squeal with delight as a cheerful family tosses chocolate bars out of their manure spreader.

"I remember that first night, lying awake while Connor snored beside me," she says. "There wasn't any magical transformation. Nothing changed between us, it just became more permanent. We're not good together, Funk. That's the truth of it. Can't spend any amount of time in the same room without fighting. If it wasn't for the kids ..."

She throws her hands up in the air. "I'm not saying what your mom did was right, but I won't lie. I understand that urge to run away and start again somewhere new. Live your life for yourself."

Neth sat with me this morning before I crashed on her couch. Stroked my hair as I told her about dinner and the shoebox and the feed mill. A part of me wants to offer a rebuttal, insist there's no justification for what Loreena did. But I can't. Not to Neth. If my best friend deserves better than this, how can I say my mother didn't?

"Have you ever thought about calling it quits with Connor?" I ask.

Neth scoffs and takes a sip of coffee. "Yeah, sure. Everyone in town already thinks I'm a fuck up. You want me to add divorcée and single mom to the list?"

"Well, you'd always have a place with me, Chicky."

"Look, don't take this the wrong way Funk," Neth says, setting down her drink, "but how long are you really going to stick around this time? Sure, your uncle is an asshole, but you could find another buyer for that place, easy."

"What, so you want me gone now too?" I joke.

"Of course not! I love having you here. But if I had a chance like yours to get out of Newfield? I wouldn't think twice about it. Especially if my whole family seemed to want me gone."

"Okay," I say, "I admit I may have gotten a little hyperbolic earlier. I'll reach out to Abe and Deb, I just need a little time. Yesterday was a surprise, but what did it really change? Loreena's gone and she's not coming back. Those postcards were just an attempt to assuage her guilt or, I don't know, her way of telling me she was going to be okay. Hoping I would be too.

"I've got a complicated history with this town, but this time I feel less alone. Maybe the retreat centre can help me change things, just by being here and not hiding who I am. I feel really close to something good. I don't want to lose it now."

Neth considers me for a moment. Her kids come running up the driveway, eager to show us their candy haul. A smile spreads across her face before she turns to them.

"That's great you guys," she says, easing out of her chair with a groan. "Why don't you grab a sucker for the road."

"Is Uncle Isaac coming with us?" asks the six-year-old.

"Absolutely, buddy!" I say, snagging a Tootsie Roll and popping it into my mouth amid playful protest. "Wouldn't miss it."

We sort out everyone's sunscreen and shoelaces, then make our way to Main Street. The kids maintain an elliptical orbit around their mother, dashing off to grab a snack from their favourite food booths, then zipping back to us with sticky fingers and peals of laughter. It pains me to give the rollkuchen such a wide berth, but I don't want to risk running into my uncle right now, so I console myself with a couple of farmer sausage burgers from the credit union instead.

Church ladies buzz around the NMC booth in coordinated chaos, depositing pails of komstborscht for the hungry masses and taking an empty one back home so they can wash and reuse it next year. Each full pail is dumped into a custom-made stockpot, which is basically a sanitized oil drum secured over a couple of propane burners. Once heated through, the conglomeration of cabbage soup is passed out to the waiting lineup in Styrofoam coffee cups topped with a buttered bun.

The queen of this impressive dance stands in front of the pot wearing a floral print apron over her clothes and a kerchief on her head to keep the hair out of her eyes. She wields a repurposed canoe paddle to stir the borscht in broad, methodical strokes. With each pass, powerful muscles ripple under the loose skin of her wrinkled arms. She must be absolutely broiling that close to the fire, but you wouldn't know it to look at her. She's a straight up, old-school Oma. Doesn't even break a sweat. Something about the way she's standing there, giving zero fucks about the line and the steam and the sun in her eyes is so beautiful it makes me want to cry.

When we're done eating, Neth buys some tickets to the carnival rides. I take the kids on all their favourites for hours: bumper cars, Tilt-A-Whirl, the Zipper. Neth watches us from the sidelines, smiling and waving whenever we come into view. By some small miracle, nobody drops their ice cream or hurls chunks or throws a tantrum. All in all, it's a perfect day.

When the country singer on the main stage gives us all a ten-minute warning, we buy a few glowsticks for the kids and unfold a picnic blanket on the grassy ditch across from the school. At precisely ten o'clock, Manitoba Hydro cuts power to all the streetlights and the town is plunged into darkness. Someone lights a fuse. The first firework screams into the sky and bursts into dazzling gold sparks that disappear just as the next one explodes into brilliant red. Everyone oohs and aahs.

As the smoke from the show begins to dissipate a few minutes later, I realize Neth's six-year-old is already asleep in my lap. Neth laughs when she sees us and raises her phone to take a picture. Then she pauses.

"That's weird," she says. "I just missed a call."

"From who?"

She shrugs and swipes through to her voicemail. Her face grows more and more concerned as the message goes on.

"Is everything okay?" I ask when she hangs up.

She won't look at me.

"Was it Connor?"

Why won't she look at me?

"Neth!"

"Just listen."

She can't get the phone out of her hand fast enough.

"Hello, Aganetha? This is Deborah Funk calling."

Deb's voice is deadpan and rough, every other word catching in her throat. It sends my heart hurtling into my stomach like a heavy stone, acid splashing up to dissolve me from the inside out.

"I'm sorry to call you so late, but I'm wondering if my nephew is with you? There's been a—it's his father."

Deb pauses to let out something between a cough and a sob before continuing.

"Abe tried to take his own life last night. He's in hospital now. It's quite serious. I've been trying to reach Isaac all day, but he isn't picking up. If you get this and he's with you, could you ask him to check his phone please and call me back? I don't know what else to—anyway. Thank you. I have to go."

20

Deb comes to pick me up in Opa's truck. She's trying to explain about last night, but I can't take it all in. Her words flash before me like the distant yard lights of farms as we make our way out of town. Swallowed by the dark just as soon as they appear.

Deb took him home from dinner.

She had a feeling.

Stayed overnight.

He waited until she was asleep.

She didn't hear the garage door open.

The jug of wiper fluid was completely drained.

The vomiting woke her up.

It felt like forever before the ambulance came.

"Isaac?"

The world fuzzes back into focus. Somehow, we're parked in front of the farmhouse.

"Why are we here?" I ask. "I want to see Abe."

Deb's shoulders slump. Her face is a web of worry lines that weren't there yesterday. "I know kid. Me too. We'll go as soon as visiting hours open tomorrow."

"That's bullshit! Just take me to St. Stache. I'll crawl through a window if I have to."

"Abe's not in St. Stache. He needs dialysis to help his kidneys get rid of the methanol, so they transferred him to Health Sciences Centre."

There's not enough air inside the truck. I tear off my seatbelt and career onto Opa's porch swing. Deb joins me, shaking out a couple of cigarettes for us. We light up and slowly rock back and forth until my chest stops heaving.

"How bad is it?" I can't get my voice above a whisper.

Deb empties her lungs with a deep sigh. "It's bad. But I called 911 as soon as I found him. They gave him charcoal and put a tube down his throat to help him breathe when he went unconscious. We should know soon how well he's responding to treatment, and they'll call if anything changes. But whatever happens, I'm here for you, okay? We'll get through this together."

She tries to offer an encouraging smile, but when I look at her, we quickly collapse into tears, holding each other as our bodies excise wave after wave of gut-twisting sobs.

Eventually, we separate. I ask if Jake and Gina know. Deb nods. "Left them a message, same as you."

"I can't believe I was such an asshole at dinner. There was nothing in that box worth fighting over. He was probably just trying to protect me. Let me hold onto the fantasy mom I'd built up in my head. I shouldn't have let Gina get to me like that."

"That's all in the past now," Deb says. "None of us were at our best last night."

"But I should have kept my mouth shut," I push back as the knot of guilt around my heart tightens. "I knew Abe was struggling. I pushed him over the edge. This is all my fault."

"Hey, hey. Hold on a minute. Look at this, will you? Tell me what you see."

Deb hands me a creased photo from her wallet. A young man with a shaggy mop of feathered blond hair is leaning into a station wagon, trying to push it out of a mucky field. Although his clothes and face are caked in mud, he's grinning from ear to ear.

"Is that—?"

"Your dad, yeah! Summer of seventy-nine. Newfield's one and only rock festival."

A small hiccup of laughter escapes between my sniffles. "You're shitting me."

"Am not. In fact, Abe's the one who organized it."

I sit in bewildered silence as Deb recounts the story. One of my father's classmates got real sick during his grade twelve year. There was an experimental drug that could help but it wasn't covered by the province or private insurance yet, so Abe decided to hold a fundraiser. It was the ten-year anniversary of Woodstock and one of Jake's university buddies was in a popular local band. Somehow, my father convinced Opa to let him hold a one-day music festival at Wonder World. Jake got a dozen bands on board, Deb helped her brother put posters up around town and in the city, and his classmates fanned out across Mennoland to sell the tickets, which were priced at two dollars.

Although Abe made sure to market the event as a fundraiser, the elders at NMC were furious. They demanded Opa Willie put a stop to the sinful gathering, and when he wouldn't, they banned him from church. Prayer meetings were held for the wayward youth bringing sex, drugs, and rock-n-roll to the town's doorstep. The good Christian business owners of Newfield were told to close up shop the day of the festival. The RCMP even canvassed the streets, telling people to keep their doors locked and their children at home.

This notoriety only increased interest in the event, however. That morning, the sun rose bright and clear. The farm's parking lot filled up in a few minutes, and soon traffic was backed up all the way to Winnipeg. Abe had been hoping to sell a few hundred tickets, but thousands of people poured into town, abandoning their cars in Opa's fields or along the highway and walking the rest of the way to the main stage. Many bypassed the ticket stalls. Jake was furious and tried to chase people down, but then Abe got the bright idea to pass feed buckets through the crowd like offering plates. Everyone ended up having a wonderful time, until the storm came.

The clouds began to gather around noon. Just after two p.m., the sky split open with a peal of thunder and the farm was quickly swamped with rain. Hail pelted down soon after, sending everyone diving for cover. People tried to leave, but the ditches were flooded and many of their cars were stuck in the mud. Jake wanted to charge a fee to help them out, but Opa just laughed at him and backed his tractor out of the barn. Though the elders tried to claim the storm was divine retribution, Oma's Kitchen quietly opened up to offer the soaked multitudes a hot meal and the Co-op called around to organize a tow truck brigade. When Opa walked into church next Sunday, nobody told him to go home.

"Abe looks like he's enjoying himself."

"Oh, he was!" Deb says. "He and his friends must have helped close to thirty cars out of the mud, and they kept joking and carrying on the whole time. Nothing got him down that day, not the traffic jams or the freeloaders or the rain. That's why I like to keep this photo close to me. Reminds me why I keep fighting for my brother in the dark times. To help him find his way back to moments like these.

"I haven't been honest with you, kid. Your dad's battled depression for a long time, longer than you've been alive. In fact, I snapped this photo less than a month before he tried to take his own life for the first time."

All these things the old man held for me, thinking he could keep me safe. It's overwhelming.

"His friend died then?" I ask. "The one he held the fundraiser for?"

"Lord, no! Full recovery. The money was more than enough to cover the drugs, so Abe made a donation to the St. Stache hospital too. That's what I'm trying to tell you. This isn't about you or me or anyone else. Your dad has carried this pain inside his whole life. He may be quiet about it, but he's one of the bravest people I know."

"Have there been other attempts?"

Deb doesn't flinch. "Yes. In seminary, and again about a year before you were born. I know it might be hard to imagine now, but he was considered a real breath of fresh air when he got hired on at the church. Abe loved that job, but it was stressful as hell, and it cost him.

"Loreena, your Opa, and I were the only people he told, because no one could know the pastor was struggling, right? For years he wouldn't even go to counselling because he was afraid he might see someone he knew in the waiting room. He swore the three of us to secrecy. I only agreed on the condition he call me whenever the walls were closing in, and I believe for the most part he did. This last while, though, it's been really bad. Worse than I've ever seen. Jake found out and made Abe take that leave of absence. Then Dad died. I think the fall in the garage really was just a fall, but I've been worried about him this whole year. I wasn't exactly surprised when last night happened. Not that it makes it any easier."

Headlights slow along the highway and swing into our lane. I notice for the first time there are other cars sitting in the old Wonder World lot. Deb sees the question on my face and explains that Triple L folks have been coming by the farm all day, holding an impromptu vigil for Abe.

"Why?" I ask. "They don't even know him."

"No," she responds, "but they know us."

She says there's food and beer and a bonfire out back, that she's thinking about joining them for a while and it's very laid-back, but they'll all understand if I prefer to go up to my room. If it were any other group of people, I might have done just that. But who knows more about loss and alienation and perseverance and hope than a bunch of small-town queers?

There are about a dozen people sitting around the fire. Everyone offers me a warm smile as I approach the circle, but they let me keep to myself. There is no performative teeth gnashing, no thinly veiled judgements wrapped in prayer. Instead, Sandy hands me a beer and I grab a bench with Deb and we all stare into the dancing flames while Jo strums a guitar and softly sings some k.d. lang with Chantal. Dupps is splayed out on her lap, purring loudly as she scratches his belly. At some point Deb's phone goes off and we all tense up, but it's just Pearl asking if she can bring us anything now that her shift has ended at the Villa.

"That's very kind of you," Deb replies, "but we'll be calling it a night soon."

I accept a couple hugs and hang-in-theres as the group disperses. Jo tells us not to worry about the farm, that they'll make sure the animals and garden are looked after for the next few days. Deb wipes her leaking eyes on her sleeve before thanking her friend.

"We're all here for you day or night, hey?" Jo says. "You need anything at all, you just holler."

Weariness places its heavy hand on our shoulders as the last car drives away, but Deb and I keep feeding logs into the fire, unable to sleep.

"You know, most days I don't miss religion," I say, staring up into the twinkling midnight sky. "It's amazing how good it feels to stop squishing every passing thought and desire through some external morality filter and just listen to your heart. But right now? I wouldn't mind tossing all my feelings at some big strong sky daddy and let him carry the weight awhile."

Deb laughs. "Well, I'm not Jesus, kid, but I'm sure here for you."

I lean into her, and she holds me gently, like my skin is a thousand shards of crumbling pottery she's doing her best to keep together.

"How did you do it?" I ask her. "Stay here all these years?"

She shrugs. "Why does anyone stay anywhere? I found my people, plain and simple. Once I had them, it was easy to ignore the naysayers who wanted me to believe I didn't belong. Newfield's my home just as much as it's Jake's or your father's. Nobody can tell me any different."

"Hey Deb?" I say, sitting up. "I want you to know that I meant what I said at dinner. Not the fuck you part, but the retreat centre. If you're up for it."

"It's late, kid," she says, checking her watch. "We can talk about this later."

"Oh, for sure, I just—I wanted you to know I was serious. And I think your people could be my people too, maybe? If you'll have me."

Fire flickers across my aunt's face, lighting up her broad smile. "Absolutely kid. We always got room for one more."

For the next few days, I spend every moment I can in the city, watching over Abe. Gradually, the hospital staff unhook him from some of his machines, which they assure me is a good sign. I'm there when he finally wakes up. When he starts breathing on his own again. He doesn't say anything, not at first, so I just sit in the room as he lies there and together we stare at the ceiling. I want him to know I can wait until he's ready. That I'm not going anywhere.

When he does finally speak, the words gurgle up from his throat like fresh rain flowing through a dry creek bed.

"You are. Still here."

"Yes," I say, taking his hand in mine. "And so are you."

I wait for him to respond, but he is silent again.

"Oh sorry, I missed my cue to say 'Praise the Lord,' didn't I?"

Abe smiles, and a tear rolls down his cheek. His hand grips mine with a fierce tenderness.

"Soo jeit et," he says.

We stay like that a long time.

Epilogue

Winnipeg in late March is a snotty nose, all slushy discharge and crusty concrete. Traffic on the 59 slows to a crawl before I've even reached the outskirts. Snow is still falling every week or two, but in between, the thermometer teases us with higher temperatures. All this thawing and rehardening has people on edge. We've put in our time like good Prairie folk. We deserve our spring.

I only remember that I need to fill up Opa's half-tonne when I see the Countryside Co-op sign in Sage Creek. A guy in an SUV behind me leans on his horn as I judder across the ruts of polished ice that pass for lanes and make a quick turn.

"Yeah, yeah, I know," I mutter under gritted teeth. "Menno driver."

I ignore the *No Cellphones* sign at the pump and call Abe to tell him I won't have time to pick him up for tonight's big event. The wiper fluid permanently damaged his vision, and while he's not completely blind, he has given up on driving. We sold the Taurus to some sixteen-year-old kid just before her MPI test. We heard afterwards she was so excited she forgot to put the car in park at the end of her test drive and crunched into a concrete planter on Main Street. Abe just smiled when he heard the news and said now the front bumper would match the back.

"Yes, I know, Deb telephoned already. I've got a ride with Maureen and her wife," he says, barely hesitating on the final word.

Abe's been spending a lot of time with the Newfield United minister lately. Maureen helped him weather the fallout when news of his latest suicide attempt inevitably spread around town. She, Deb, and I were all in the front row the day he addressed his congregation to share the full truth about his lifelong struggle with depression. A church meeting was held later that afternoon and the membership surprised us by voting to keep Abe on as their pastor, though a disgruntled faction did leave NMC to start their own church. In the end, most folks appreciated their pastor's candour. Some even spoke up about their own mental health challenges, sparking an important and overdue conversation in town.

"Sounds good," I say. "Can I take you home afterwards, shovel your driveway?"

"Too late! Took care of that first thing this morning."

I give him a good-natured scolding for this. I've been telling him to take it easy and let me help out more ever since he got back from the hospital, but I can't really complain about his newfound energy. It took a few more tries, but Abe and his doctor found the right antidepressant for him in the end.

A pump attendant walks out to help another car, but frowns when he sees me on my phone. He points at the sign.

"Shit, I've got to go, see you later?"

"Drive safe son," Abe says.

"Yeah, okay, and don't forget to bring cash tonight!"

I make my way down Lagimodiere to Regent, the Mint sparkling in the late afternoon sun like a palace carved out of ice. Maneuvering a Hummer-sized cart through Costco's Kirkland Signature Nine Circles of Hell, I do my best to gather up everything on my last-minute shopping list. Napkins, drink cups, and ice-melter for me. Diapers, yogurt cups, and ice-melter for Neth. She's had a lot on her plate ever since she found out Connor was cheating on her with Steph P. and kicked him to the curb. Uncle Isaac has been running errands, cooking KD, and settling squabbles between the older two kiddos so Neth can focus on her new baby.

Every other waking moment I have has been spent working on the farm. The cabins won't be ready until the summer, but we've already got our first reservation: a queer and trans youth camp out from the city. We're also planning to fix up the old petting zoo area. Ever since that yoga with goats video went viral, we've received multiple inquiries from fitness enthusiasts looking to add a bit of the barnyard to their workout routine. I'm sure somewhere, Opa's laughing.

Tonight, we're hosting our very first event in the renovated barn space. When Deb and I first announced our plans to revamp Wonder World, we got a sterile two sentence acknowledgement in the *Notes from Newfield* section of *The Weekly Word* on page seventeen. They sandwiched us between a report on a hog barn fire and a very detailed account of Mrs. Irene Unrau's successful bunion surgery. I laughed off their disinterest, but someone in the city must have seen the news, because suddenly CBC and *The Free Press* were asking for interviews. After those articles came out, I heard from a lot of my high school's queer and trans alum. The messages all sounded very similar to one another. *I thought I was alone. I thought I couldn't stay. Thank you for making a place I can come back to.*

Not everyone's been supportive of course. I get a lot of looks whenever I shop in town, and I've heard rumours there might be a protest planned for tonight. I say if people want to freeze their asses off while we're having a good time, let them. The queers are here to stay in Mennoland. We aren't going to be the quiet in the land anymore.

The lines are long at Costco, so I'm even later to my final stop in the city. Tonight's guest of honour doesn't seem to mind, though. A flurry of fringe and gold sequins glides towards the truck, six-inch heels navigating the icy sidewalk with ease.

"Hello, darling!" I say, kissing the air around her cheeks. "You look sickening."

"Nothing but the best for my first hometown gig."

It took me a week and a few stiff drinks to gather my courage and open the email I received from Noah Enns three months ago. I don't know what I was expecting when I saw his name in the retreat centre's inbox, but it definitely wasn't a photo of him in full drag.

Noah told me he'd left the Mennonite Disaster Service two years ago and came out to his family soon after. Most of them stopped speaking to him, including his parents, which was hard, but not as hard as it might have been without his new queer friends in Winnipeg. When Prairie Theatre Exchange announced a Drag 101 class last spring, Noah jumped at the chance and Anna Baptiste, his fabulous alter ego, was born.

He said he was happy to hear I was back in Manitoba and that he hoped I was doing well. He also said he was very sorry for the way he acted when Abe brought us before the elders. That he was cowardly and immature and totally unfair to me. He didn't make excuses or ask for my forgiveness but offered to take me out for a beer if I was ever interested in reconnecting no pressure thanks again have a good one. I dialled the number at the bottom of the page as soon as I finished reading his message.

"I'll go for drinks with you on one condition," I said. "Come by the farm when it's ready for visitors. Newfield needs your drag."

The queen lets out a joyful screech when we pull up to the farm's new sign, a massive timber frame arch lit by multicoloured spotlights and flanked by the pride and trans flags, a gift from Newfield United.

"Welcome to Funk-Ups Farm Retreat!" I say.

"Bitch, it looks stunning!" Anna Baptiste pronounces, smacking my arm with her acrylics.

"Yeah, well, us queers know how to handle our power tools."

"Damn right!"

Anna's show doesn't start for another hour, but the parking lot is already half full. I usher her into the barn's side entrance before getting Jo to help me unload the rest of her gear and my Costco supplies. Deb and I want to hire back all the Triple L folks we can. So far, Jo's been a great handyworker and self-proclaimed bigot bouncer, and soon they'll be helping Deb expand our orchard and gardens. By the end of the year, folks will be able to sign up for medicine walks, foraging trips, and canning workshops with them as well.

"How's it going in there?" I ask.

"Real good, yep!"

"Any sign of trouble tonight?"

"Naw," Jo says, shaking their head. "Not a peep."

"Halleloo."

Inside the barn, strings of fairy lights draped around the rafters cast the growing crowd in a warm glow. Deb waves at me from behind the kitchen, where she seems to be doing a steady sale of drinks and snacks. On stage, Chantal is playing some chill hangout music, her mellow voice floating over the excited buzz of conversation in the room. When I told her my plans for Wonder World, she insisted on buying me an old piano from MCC. She and Jo hauled it out to the farm and got it retuned. Together, we sanded it down and painted it bright gold. With her encouragement I've even been playing again, a little. Old hymns and pop songs, whatever comes to mind. I'm rusty, sure, but perfection isn't the goal. Persistence is. For the first time in a long time, the keys feel right under my fingers.

When everything's ready, I signal Chantal and she hands the mic over to me.

"Hello everyone. Welcome to our very first live event at Funk-Ups Farm Retreat!"

The crowd roars its approval.

"Now, before we begin, I would like to—and I can't believe I'm saying this—invite the mayor of Newfield to say a few words."

More cheers follow as Pearl takes the stage in a silvery tuxedo and top hat. Uncle Jake shocked the whole town when he announced his resignation from council not long after his plans for Riverview Terrace fell through. Apparently, his investors weren't too happy and wanted him gone. Their efforts to replace him with a hasty byelection failed, however, when Pearl put her hat in the ring. During the campaign, she set herself apart from the establishment candidate by actually speaking to voters and offering thoughtful responses to the issues they raised. A lot of people were set in their ways or chose to stay home on election day, but in the end, she won by eighty-three votes. The retreat centre has had a strong ally in the town office ever since, and her staff have certainly appreciated the chance to share the thermostat controls with their new boss.

"Wow," Pearl says, "look at all of you beautiful people! Newfield really turned it out tonight. I just want to say how happy I am to be here with you. As your mayor, I will do everything in my power to make our town a welcoming place for everyone. I think Deb and Isaac Funk have an important role to play in that work and I can't wait to join you here again for all of the wonderful events they have planned."

A gust of cold air from the entrance draws my attention, and I turn to greet our latest guest.

"Hi Abe."

"I brought cash," he says, glancing around uncertainly. "What do I do with it?"

"It's for tips," I say with a laugh. "Just put your hand out during one of Anna's songs. She'll take it from you."

The old man was a little nervous when I explained Ms. Baptiste would be entertaining us this evening, but I assured him I'd checked in ahead of time and confirmed she was cool with him being there. I was glad about that because I'm kind of hoping Noah will be around more often. Not that I'm trying to rush anyone into anything.

The lights go down and the opening bars of "Like a Virgin" play over the sound system. I let out a hoot and guide my father closer to the stage. Abe handles his first drag show pretty well. He holds up a fresh twenty during "Man! I Feel Like a Woman!" and chuckles to himself when Anna Baptiste offers a kiss of thanks in return. The outline of her lips stays on his forehead the rest of the night.

Hours later, after everyone's gone home, I find Neth sprawled out on the bearskin rug in Opa's taxidermy room. Dupps is snuggled in beside her, purring loudly.

"I can't believe you're getting rid of all these guys," she says, somehow knowing it's me without opening her eyes.

"I could always set some aside for you," I offer. "I bet Connor would think twice about dropping by for another drunken tirade if we station the tigers outside your front door."

Neth shrieks with laughter.

"Perfect, load up the minivan!"

"You got it, Chicky. Do you know how proud I am of you?"

"Yeah, yeah," she says with a groan. "I'm freaking Wonder Woman. Can I stay over tonight? I think I overdid it a little."

"For sure, I'll make up the couch. Do you need me to get in touch with anyone for you?"

"Nope. I knew you'd say yes so I texted my mom already. If I call home now, the kids are just going to want to unload Oma's latest children's bible trauma on me and I am so not here for that right now."

There's a knock at the front door.

"Uh, hey, can I tell you something?" I ask Neth.

"Yeah."

"Promise not to make a big deal out of it?"

"Just spill the beans!"

"Okay, well, there might be an extra person around the breakfast table in the morning. So, I just want you to be prepared in case that happens, okay? And don't be weird."

Neth sits up with a flail of her arms, sending Dupps skittering out of the room.

"Isaac Funk! Are you telling me that's a booty call out there?"

"Neth, be cool."

"I'm cool, okay? But what are you still doing here? Go get your cute human, dude!"

The knocking comes again, louder this time. I rush down the hallway and open the door just as Abe and Deb poke their heads out of the kitchen. Perfect.

"Noah!" the old man calls out. "That was quite the show. Never seen anything like it."

"Glad you enjoyed yourself Mr. Funk," Noah says, his freshly scrubbed face shiny with moisturizer.

"It was really great," Deb echoes. "We'd love to have you again."

"Oh, definitely!"

We stand there in awkward silence for a moment before Noah clears his throat.

"Right," I say. "So, anyway, we should probably ... uh, Abe, did you still need a ride home?"

"It's alright kid," Deb says with a wink. "I got it."

"Okay, cool. Well, Noah and I are going to stay here then."

Abe reaches for his coat. Noah steps inside and I lean against him ever so slightly. The tips of his fingers brush against mine, making me shiver.

The old man pauses at the door, and to my surprise he reaches out to shake both of our hands.

"It was nice to see you again, Noah," he says. "You boys have a lovely evening."

And we do.

Acknowledgements

There are so many people whose kindness, wisdom, and encouragement brought *Wonder World* into being. Through beach walks and shared pots of tea, my spouse Marie Raynard and our dearest friends Holli and Marissa Joy gave me the courage to nurture and expand my earliest ideas into a fully fledged manuscript. Raynard my love, thank you for sharing this journey with me and walking beside me every step of the way.

Beth Carlson-Malena, Stephanie Klassen, and Erin Koop Unger offered valuable insights on rough drafts of this story, and countless family members, friends, and friendly strangers were gracious enough to consult with me on a variety of research topics. My editor Catharina de Bakker offered enthusiastic support for this project from the very beginning. Her thoughtful questions and comments helped me go further and deeper into Isaac's world than I ever could have on my own. My most heartfelt thanks to the whole team at Enfield & Wizenty for championing this complicated queer love letter to the Prairies.

I was incredibly fortunate to participate in both the Writers' Federation of Nova Scotia's Alistair MacLeod Mentorship Program and the Banff Centre's Emerging Writers Intensive during *Wonder World*'s development. As a first-time novelist, I couldn't have asked for better mentors than Jacqueline Dumas at WFNS and Joshua Whitehead at the Banff Centre. This story and my entire writing practice have been truly transformed by their generous feedback, reassurance, and overall life advice. My Banff Centre cohort became fast friends and creative collaborators, and I send much love and gratitude to Betty Ann Adam, Jennilee Austria, Jan Guenther Braun, Hali Heavy Shield, Rhonda Gladue, Sam K. MacKinnon, and Omar Ramirez. I would also like to thank the Canada Council for the Arts for supporting the novel's revision process with a Research and Creation grant.

While writing this book, I was a guest in Indigenous territories across Turtle Island including Treaty 1, the traditional lands of the Anishinaabeg, Cree, Oji-Cree, Dakota, and Dene Peoples, and the homeland of the Métis Nation; Treaty 7, the traditional lands of the Stoney Nakoda Nations of Wesley, Chiniki, and Bearspaw, three Nations of the Blackfoot Confederacy: the Pikani, Kainai, and Siksika, and the Tsuu T'ina of the Dene People, that is also shared with the Métis Nation of Alberta, Region III; and Mi'kma'ki, the ancestral and unceded territory of the Mi'kmaq People. As a child, I participated in a ceremony recognizing the longstanding relationship between Mennonites and the Métis as part of the 2002 Red River Métis Journey. I'm grateful to the Elders and Knowledge Keepers I met that day for starting me down a pathway of learning about, and reckoning with, the ways in which prairie settlers have relied on both the assistance and exploitation of First Nations and Métis Peoples to establish our communities within Indigenous territories. In telling the story of *Wonder World*, I think it is important to acknowledge this truth.

Invidia Obscura

K.R. Byggdin grew up on the Prairies and now lives on the East Coast. They are currently completing studies in English and Creative Writing at Dalhousie University. Their writing has appeared in anthologies and journals across Canada, the UK, and New Zealand. *Wonder World* is their first novel.